RETURN OF THE GUNMEN

RETURN OF THE GUNMEN

by

Jim Bowden

Dales Large Print Books
Long Preston, North Yorkshire,
BD23 4ND, England.

British Library Cataloguing in Publication Data.

Bowden, Jim
    Return of the gunmen.

      A catalogue record of this book is
      available from the British Library

      ISBN   978-1-84262-820-1 pbk

First published in Great Britain 1988 by Robert Hale Limited

Copyright © Jim Bowden 1988

Cover illustration © Michael Thomas

The moral right of the author has been asserted

Published in Large Print 2011 by arrangement with
Mr W. D. Spence

Dales Large Print is an imprint of Library Magna Books Ltd.

Printed and bound in Great Britain by
T.J. (International) Ltd., Cornwall, PL28 8RW

One

Cap Millet licked his parched lips, dry from anxiety and tension rather than from the heat of the sun which scorched the dusty town of Pine Bluffs. His hand around the Colt 45 felt clammy and the pit of his stomach churned and knotted.

He was alone in the sheriff's office and somewhere outside, among the board buildings, were four men who had sworn that he would not see nightfall. Four men, all smart with a gun, while his help was confined to a twenty-year-old deputy who still had to fire a gun in anger, and he was out of town.

The showdown, the challenge, had come sooner than he had expected. That it had to come sometime had become certain this last week.

Clayton Foster had the town in his pocket.

The few people who had stood up to him had gradually diminished through fear of the consequences or because they saw the situation as being hopeless of retrieval.

They accepted Foster's authority, turned a blind eye to his rackets and lived peacefully or they left Pine Bluffs. Few wanted to do that as this was their home and most had been here before Foster. They condoned his ways and lived in peace, willing to agree by not protesting, taking the easy way out and by so doing lost the soul of their town.

Foster had come with money, bought the Golden Cage and revamped it to attract more custom. Word spread and men rode into Pine Bluffs for their pleasure. Cattle drovers used it as a relaxation before they pressed on across the townless stretch to the Red River. Drink flowed, gaming tables were crowded and more girls were readily available. They all made money for Clay Foster who used it to buy out the local newspaper, the hotel, and other desirable property which channelled more wealth into his bank account. But his eyes were set on greater pickings and it was only a fortnight ago that Cap had found out the real reason behind Foster's latest interest – land to the south of the town.

Cap had come to Pine Bluffs at the request of an old family friend, Mal Porter, who did not like the way the town was being taken over. When the sheriff, who took the easy way out by succumbing to Foster's bribes, had died, Mal seized the opportunity to try to save his beloved town. Seeming to play along with Foster, he had managed to persuade him to agree to Cap's appointment as sheriff, having warned Cap of the situation.

When he met opposition to his attempt to buy land to the south of Pine Bluffs from two ranchers, Foster brought in four gunmen. Murmurings of protest ebbed among some townsfolk but no one dared move, the presence of the gunmen quelled any spirit which might ignite.

Cap realised that the time for action had come and he revealed his true position at a clandestine meeting of possible supporters, arranged by Mal, but he soon recognised that his attempt to turn the protests into action against Foster were of no avail.

'I'm not setting my life up for the town,' said one. 'I've a wife and kids,' pointed out another. 'If my old lady knew I was here, she'd skin me. Stay out of trouble, she warned,' said another. 'Foster's brought money to the town, trade's good.'

Only his deputy, Richie Collins, a raw youngster to whom Cap had taken a liking, and Mal backed Cap.

Now Cap faced a gunfight alone. Richie was out of town and Mal – well, Cap had warned him to stay out of the way. As much as the older man was willing to buckle on a gun-belt in support of Cap, the lawman knew he would be no match for the professional gun-slingers. Besides, he wanted Mal to come to no harm for Laura's sake.

She was devoted to her father and they had become particularly close after her mother's death when she was thirteen. Now, twenty years later, a bonny, mature woman, she feared for her father's safety. She had found some measure of relief with Cap's arrival.

She had taken to the tall, lean man immediately she had seen him swinging slowly from the saddle in a smooth, lithe movement in front of her house at the west end of the main street. There was an air about him which instilled a confidence, a feeling that now everything would be all right.

When she had greeted him she had felt a gentle firmness in his handshake. She saw in his gaunt look the marks of a troubled past. His eyes bore a sadness and she knew this man had suffered. She had the story from her father of how Cap, returning from the War between the States, learned of his wife's rape and murder, of how he had eventually tracked down her killers and wreaked a terrible revenge. After which he had drifted.

Until now. A future of drifting had been banished in Pine Bluffs. Cap had been captivated by the gentle, pretty woman who had opened the door to him. Her greeting was warm, her smile friendly. There was a deep sincerity in her light blue eyes which told Cap she meant it when she returned the love he professed for her after a month of seeing a great deal of each other.

But neither was blind to the real purpose of his being in Pine Bluffs and that there could be an outcome which would shatter their plans of a ranch in Montana. They did not voice their fear and they made preparations to leave once Pine Bluffs had found its true self again. But they had not reckoned on Cap facing four gunmen alone.

Cap moved across his office to the side of the window and peered out cautiously. The main street was quiet. No one moved. The scene was unnatural. The town was hung on an expectancy. There was a tension of people standing on the brink of an eruption which could overwhelm every one of them and yet they were not prepared to prevent it.

The sun seared the street, burning its influence into the taut atmosphere. Cap blinked against the glare, tipped his stetson off his forehead and wiped the beads of sweat away with the back of his hand. He glanced at the mahogany-framed clock on the wall to the right of his desk. The numerals were stark against the white face and the pointers not only showed the time but indicated that there was no stopping the coming of a showdown. The brass pendulum swung ceaselessly, behind its glass cover, with the certainty that time would catch up with everyone and that for Cap that time could be near.

Cap frowned at the timekeeper. Hell, he was letting things get on his nerves. He stiffened. There was a time when in such a situation he would have been ice cool. He had faced his wife's killers with a certainty of the outcome which had made his mind sharp, razorlike in its assessment of each little incident in every situation. But now? Cap cursed himself. Now there was Laura, living, vibrant. Laura who had stirred feelings in him which he had never expected to sense again. But the fact that she was there, that he wanted her for the rest of a long, long future was raising in him an over-anxiety to be successful and a realisation that the odds were stacked against him.

He drew sharply on his breath. This was no good. This was no way to face four professional guns who had sworn to kill him. He must do something. He must not be caught cooped-up in his office. But where were they?

Step outside the front door and he could be blasted from any quarter. Use the back way and the narrowness of the alley could make him a certain victim for there would be no cover from a gunman stationed at either end of the alley. There was only the trap door in the ceiling of the store-room at the back of the building. That could give him a chance but he would like some idea where the gunmen were before he moved.

Cap waited, watching the main street.

The clock pointers moved on. Five minutes. Ten minutes. The town remained still.

Fifteen minutes. Tension heightened. Cap felt eyes on him. Twenty minutes. Nothing moved.

The flash came so suddenly and was gone in the same instant that, although he was startled by it, Cap almost believed it had never happened. Then, just as suddenly, it was there again and gone again. Cap was alert. Every nerve strained. A signal meant for him? It must be. Or was it a ruse to divert his attention from some other movement – someone closing in on the sheriff's office? It came again. Cap caught its place of origin. Kate Robson's room on the first floor of the Golden Cage.

Richie! It had to be. He must be back in town. The odds were shortened.

Though Kate worked for Clayton Foster she did not agree with his ways and only tolerated him because he paid her well to run his saloon. Cap, on coming to Pine Bluffs, had soon assessed the situation and had recognised that in Kate he had a good friend who could pass him useful information. It had worked to a degree and Cap was grateful. Kate had liked Cap from their first meeting and would have made a play for him but realising his true feelings lay elsewhere she accepted the fact that he would never feel for her as she did for him. Being the generous-hearted woman she was, she held no resentment and continued to value Cap's friendship.

Now, Cap figured she was showing it again. Richie must have sensed trouble when he reached town, checked it out, probably with Laura and her father, and then used the back stairs to Kate's room from where he could assess the situation at the sheriff's office. He had probably learned from her the whereabouts of Cap and was now trying to draw his attention.

Cap needed to answer. The mirror from the upper room reflected the sun again. Cap closed the shutter on his window and opened it again. He peered at the window across the street and saw a figure appear and move away.

Richie! He was right.

Cap's blood quickened. Maybe Richie had learned the whereabouts of the gunmen. Cap holstered his Colt and hurried to the store-room at the back of the office, snatching up his Winchester on the way. He positioned a chair below the trapdoor, climbed on it, reached up and pushed firmly. The wood resisted. Cap wondered when the trapdoor had last been used. It had certainly never been opened since he had come to Pine Bluffs. He pushed a little harder. He needed to be careful. If the trapdoor gave way suddenly it could create a noise which would attract the gunmen's attention and the last thing he wanted was to disclose any of his movements to them.

Cap firmed his strength against the resisting woodwork. He felt a slight yield. Extra pressure. It gave a little more. Dust showered down from the crack which was appearing round the framework. Cap exerted a little more strength. The gap widened. Daylight. Cap eased one side of the trapdoor upwards until he was able to get a firm grip on it. He pushed it carefully upwards and over, levering it on to the roof without a sound.

He thrust his rifle slowly outside and hauled himself through the hole, squirming on his stomach so that he would not be seen. He crawled across the roof until he was behind the wooden parapet overlooking main street. He removed his stetson and eased himself up slowly so that he could view Kate Robson's window situated opposite and slightly above him. No one. He stared hard. A figure moved from in the room and appeared momentarily at the window and then disappeared to one side. Richie! The curtain moved slightly. Cap hoped Richie was looking out as he made a signal with his hand.

Cap waited and watched. The curtain moved again and Cap once more raised his hand. A moment later he saw Richie standing just sufficiently back from the window so that only the man opposite the window would see him. He gesticulated. Cap read his meaning and signalled back that he had understood. Cap crawled quickly across the roof so that he could look into the alley. No one. Had Richie been wrong?

Cap cast the doubt from his mind. He knew Richie. He was competent. Though still a raw twenty, new to the role of lawman, he had a sharp brain and could assess a situation quickly. Cap had taught him to use a gun and he had learned fast though he still had to fire that gun in the course of his job. Cap was dubious about Richie's chances when he came up against the likes of Foster's hired guns, the brothers Joe, Pete and Jake Wells and their sidekick, the Cheyenne Kid.

The brothers were rough, tough and handy with their fists as well as their guns. There was something of bluster in their approach which some might put down to nervousness but Cap had soon learned that this was not so. Instead it was a rolling technique which often caught their opponents unaware that trouble was coming. The Cheyenne Kid, on the other hand, deceived with his casualness.

Behind his dreamy exterior was an alert mind which governed his eyes to miss nothing and mustered his whole being into action with a speed which completely outwitted.

Cap waited, watching in the direction indicated by Richie. Five minutes passed and Cap was beginning to get impatient. He felt he needed to precipitate some action. He couldn't just sit time out on this flat roof under the blazing sun. Should he draw attention to himself or...?

Cap's thoughts were interrupted by the faint scrape of a footstep. Every nerve in Cap's body went on the alert. Someone must have come into the alley two blocks away and was now moving quickly but stealthily in the direction of the sheriff's office.

Cap eased himself for a better view and drew his rifle to him. A figure, approaching with a quick step, Colt in hand, came into his vision. Jake Wells!

Nearing the office, Wells slowed and paused. A whistle came from somewhere on the other side of the main street and almost at the same instant the sharp crack of rifles shattered the stillness which had hung oppressively over Pine Bluffs for some time. Jake broke into a run to cover the last few yards to the rear door of the sheriff's office.

Cap read the plan. The other three gunmen were to keep him pinned down inside the office while Jake took him from the rear. In an instance he was on his feet, his rifle aimed at the figure below as he yelled, 'Hold it right there, Jake!'

Startled by the unexpected, Jake jerked to a stop, looking upwards. His Colt came up but before he could squeeze the trigger, Cap fired. Jake slammed against the wall. The disbelief in his eyes glazed as he slid to the ground and lay still.

Cap swung round, moved swiftly in a crouch across the roof, dropping to his stomach before reaching the parapet. A quick glance told him that the gunmen were firing from the cover of some barrels at the end of the alley next to the saloon. But how many? He couldn't be certain in that swift glance. He looked to Kate Robson's window. There was no sign of Richie.

Directing his gaze back to the alley he realised that he had the drop on the gunmen. Come forward and they were in the open. Move back and he still had them for he could cover the length of the alley with his rifle. Any moment they would be expecting Jake to make his kill and when nothing happened they would become suspicious and act accordingly. Cap must not let them. He must let them know that his rifle held them captive.

He eased himself into a shooting position and took careful aim over the top of the central barrel. He squeezed the trigger.

The unexpected whine of a bullet close to them startled the gunmen and cut short their firing. Cap seized that moment.

'Joe, Pete, Cheyenne!' he yelled. 'I can get you no matter which way you move!'

Shattered by the unexpected voice from the roof of the sheriff's office the gunmen hesitated.

Cap loosed off another shot over their heads to emphasise his superiority and then yelled, 'And Jake can't help you, he's dead!'

'Hell! You bastard, Millet!' The anger in the voice was followed by a volley of shots which went whining harmlessly over Cap's head.

When it ceased, Cap yelled, 'It's no use, Wells, you ain't got the right angle but I've got the drop on you, may as well give up.'

'Like hell!'

Cap noticed a movement and a figure appeared edging back along the alley. The lawman loosed off a shot over the man's head sending him scurrying back to the protection of the barrels.

'Damn you, Millet,' a voice screamed.

'Like I said, you can't move unless you come out with hands up.'

Angry shots were loosed off across the main street with little hope of them doing any good. As hard as he tried Cap could not figure out how many men were behind the barrels. Two certainly but were there three?

If not where was the third gunman? And where was Richie?

'You giving up?' called Cap.

No reply.

Silence came once more to Pine Bluffs. Men sweated out the moments.

Suddenly the sound of horse's hoofs breaking into a gallop came from the direction of the livery stable. Cap moved to get a view of the rider. Clayton Foster! There was no way he could stop him.

A man, gun in hand, moved out of one of the gardens near the end of Main Street. Mal Porter! Cap went cold.

'Get back, get back,' he yelled, but his cries were useless. Mal was too far away to hear. Cap could only stare in horror as the old man walked into the middle of the roadway with Clay Foster thundering down on him. Mal raised his arm, the gun pointing. A shot blasted above the sound of the pounding hoofs but Clay had seen Mal's intention and had swerved his horse. He swung the animal back on to its original run and before Mal could squeeze the trigger again the horse was upon him. Its powerful body sent him crashing to the ground under its flaying hoofs. Then it was past, continuing its full gallop of escape.

Whether by instinct, or some superhuman effort, Cap couldn't tell, but he saw Mal, still clutching the gun, roll over on to his stomach and take aim at Clay's back. In the same instance the Cheyenne Kid leaped the fence of a garden next to Mal's and fired twice. Mal's body jerked and he never fired that last shot.

Cap felt numb. He was sickened by his inability to do anything to save Mal. The whole thing had happened so quickly and yet it was impinged on Cap's mind as if it had all happened in slow motion. Suddenly he was aware that he had been diverted from his objective. He swung round, back to his view of the alley. He loosed off two shots. There was no reply. He stared hard and cursed. Where only a few moments ago he had been able to detect someone between the barrels, now there was only space. The Wells brothers had seized the diversion and extracted themselves from the trap in which they had been caught.

The hunt was on again. Three gunmen. Two lawmen. But where the hell was Richie?

Two

Cap surveyed the street and buildings quickly but there was no sign of the Wells brothers. They could be closing in on him, they knew his whereabouts and they would be filled with revenge now they knew he had killed Jake. He must not get caught on the open roof.

He started across the roof in a low crouch and was half-way to the trapdoor when he heard a scream which froze him. He spun round and dropped on to his stomach in a position from which he could look along the street.

In spite of the heat he went cold. The Cheyenne Kid held Laura tight round the waist with his left arm while his right hand aimed his Colt close to her side. Laura, shocked by her father's killing, must have run out of the house instinctively and in so doing had given the Cheyenne Kid a chance he was not going to ignore.

'Millet!' There was a touch of triumphant laughter in the Kid's voice. 'You hear me! Laura's dead unless you get down here without your guns.'

A cold sweat broke out on Cap's forehead. He licked his parched lips. A few moments ago he had the upper hand, now, because Mal had ignored the instructions he had been given, the whole situation had changed. Desperately Cap sought some way out of his predicament. Do as the Kid said and Cap was certain that he would not live much longer and once that news reached Foster, who must have reckoned things were going against him, he would soon return to have the town in his power.

'Millet! I know you're on the roof of your office. So don't play games, get on to the street!'

Cap did not reply.

'Millet!' Irritation had come to the Kid's

voice and with it was the cold calculation of a killer. 'You ain't got any help. Collins ain't back yet so...'

'Nice work, Cheyenne. We'll bring the bastard down.' The Wells brothers, grinning broadly, moved on to the street from the building next to the saloon and hurried towards the sheriff's office.

Cap knew he could outgun the brothers from his position but there was Laura.

As if he had read Cap's thoughts Cheyenne yelled, 'And don't try anything, Millet. I've still got Laura...'

His words were cut short by the crash of a gun.

The Kid yelled and staggered, his grip on Laura loosening. As soon as she felt his hold slacken, Laura twisted and pushed hard at him. The Kid stumbled and fell. Laura spun round and flung herself sideways towards the garden railings.

'Don't try it, Kid!' The cold warning rapped sharply from Richie Collins who stood a few yards away, his Colt levelled menacingly at the man prone on the ground, his face drawn in pain which seared from the wound in his leg. 'Throw your gun over here.'

The Kid hesitated.

'Do it!' rapped Richie.

The Kid did as he was told, cursing the fact that Richie had outplayed him and had had the sense to wait until the Wells brothers were inside the sheriff's office. He had neutralised their effectiveness because of Cap's superior position.

'Damn you!' snarled the Kid. 'Where the hell did you come from?'

'Got back sooner than expected. Heard what was happening just before I hit town. Been watching you. Pity I couldn't stop you gunning Mal. You all right, Laura?'

'Yes,' replied Laura pulling herself up by the railings.

'Better get inside. This ain't over yet,' Richie nodded towards the sheriff's office.

Laura glanced at her father's body and, with tears marking her cheeks, she hurried into the house.

'You all right, Cap?' Richie yelled.

'Sure,' the answer came back. 'Nice work. The Wells boys are sure bottled up. Hi, Joe, Pete, may as well give…'

Cap's words were cut short by the sudden blast of guns as the Wells brother ripped their shots in anger through the ceiling.

'Wells! Cheyenne's likely to bleed to death if he don't get a doc and I ain't sending for one until you come out.' Richie seeing that Cheyene was about to yell the truth about his wound menaced him with his Colt and stopped him.

'Throw your guns out and then walk out front with your hands high.' Cap's voice threatened their lives should the Wells brothers try to shoot it out. He knew they would realise that, pinned in the office, with himself on the roof and Richie on the street, their situation was hopeless. They would be easy targets if they tried to use the trap door on to the roof, they could not get a gun on Cap and, with no window to see in the direction of Richie, they could not get a line

31

on the young deputy.

There was silence.

'You don't need long to think it over,' called Cap. 'There's two choices, alive or dead.'

'Damn you, Millet,' shouted Joe Wells. 'We're coming out.'

'Right, guns first,' replied Cap. 'And take it easy 'cos I've got the drop on you.'

Cap moved quickly and quietly across the roof so that he could look down on the front of the building. He held his rifle ready.

A moment later two rifles followed by two Colts fell into the dust in front of the office.

'Hold it,' called Cap. 'One at a time. You first Joe.'

Joe Wells, arms raised, appeared on the sidewalk. He paused and glanced upwards into the muzzle of a rifle held by Cap.

'Right, Joe, on to the roadway.' Cap's voice held a threat, warning Joe of the consequences should he do anything but obey.

The gunman moved down the two steps into the dust of the street. He walked four paces before Cap called a halt.

'You now, Pete,' called Cap.

Pete followed his brother into the roadway. Once the two men were side by side, Richie motioned to Cheyenne, 'Join 'em.'

'I can't,' moaned Cheyenne. 'Not with this leg,' he added indicating his wound.

'It's only a flesh wound,' rapped Richie. 'Won't kill you to hobble to your partners.'

Cheyenne knew it was useless to argue and pushed himself gingerly to his feet. Hoping to upset Richie's vigilance, he pretended to stumble but the deputy's gun never wavered.

Cheyenne started slowly in the direction of the Wells brothers. Richie bided his time.

Cap kept a close scrutiny on Pete and Joe until the Cheyenne Kid was beside the brothers.

'Watch 'em, Richie,' called Cap as the deputy placed himself so that he had all three covered by his Colt.

'Sure,' acknowledged Richie.

Cap hurried across the roof of his office

and lowered himself through the trapdoor. A few moments later he was stepping out on to the sidewalk. He paused when he saw two men drift out of the saloon and stop to stare at the scene. Two more pushed through the batwings to join them. Then two more. Cap detected some movement along the street and casting quick glances in both directions he saw that the people of Pine Bluffs were appearing in ones and twos. He stepped off the sidewalk and as he walked to Richie he noted that the drift on to the street was gathering momentum.

Whispers became loud talk until the air was buzzing with comments about what had happened and of what it meant for the town. Along the street a small knot of people stood staring at the body of Mal Porter and at his daughter who had reappeared to kneel sobbing at her father's side.

Cap took in the whole scene with contempt and disgust. He knew the townsfolk would have been doing just the same if he and Richie had been lying in the dust. They would have been singing the praises of Clay Foster and his gunmen instead of calling the names of Cap Millet and Richie Collins as saviours of Pine Bluffs. Try as he had, he could never persuade them to help themselves. They would not oppose Foster of their own will. Get somebody else to do it and if he succeeded all well and good, if not they'd knuckle down to the ways of Foster and his sidekicks. Their pride in their town and in themselves had gone. Now they would seek excuses for their behaviour and attitude and salve their souls of any blame for what had happened. They would bring themselves to believe that if they had tried to stand up to Foster, if they had sided with the sheriff, there would have been more bloodshed. As it was only Mal Porter had been killed, and that was his own stupid fault. If he had stayed indoors and not interfered in a showdown, in which he had no place, he would still have been alive. Cap knew how the people would be thinking and he was disgusted with them.

'You and you!' he snapped suddenly, causing the two men to whom he directed his call, to start. 'Tell Doc Warren to come to my office. And the other help the undertaker with Mal.'

The two men sped off.

'Let's get 'em inside, Richie.' Cap stood to one side and motioned in the direction of his office door, with his rifle.

The gunmen shuffled reluctantly towards the steps. Richie, moving backwards in front of them, covered them with his Colt while Cap fell in behind them, his rifle ready. Richie moved into the office and as the men passed him he saw the hate in their eyes and especially in the Kid's.

'I'll get you for this,' Cheyenne hissed. 'You won't get lucky next time.'

Richie ignored the threat.

Cap stepped into the office and closed the door behind him.

People surged forward in the street and a crowd gathered outside the sheriff's office. Men, peering through the window, passed on a commentary about what was happening inside. There was a constant hum of question and answer. It grew louder as the door opened and the doctor came in, then subsided when he closed the door.

The short, moustached man peered over metal-rimmed spectacles, his eyes darting to every man in the room. 'Oh, it's you,' he said sharply, when he noted Cheyenne's wound. He glanced questioningly at the sheriff.

'Want you to patch him up fit to travel to Little Rock as soon as possible,' said Cap.

The small man grunted, placed his bag on Cap's desk and pushed his low-crowned sombrero back off his forehead. 'Sit down,' he rapped at Cheyenne.

The Kid started to move.

'Hold it!' Cap's voice was sharp and incisive. 'Wait until we've got these others in the cells.'

'Wait?' the doctor snapped. 'I can't hang about. I've got other patients to see to!'

Cap eyed him contemptuously. 'Other patients? You weren't bothered about them a short while ago.'

'What do you mean?' The doctor's eyes narrowed as he glared at the sheriff.

'You were soon here when I sent for you, I guess you were close. I figure you'd heard what was going to happen today and you hung around to see which way it went. You swim both ways, Doc, and you wanted to know which way you'd be swimming after today.'

The doctor spluttered and started to protest but Cap cut him short.

'You're as bad as the rest of them out there. There isn't one who's worth calling a man.'

'See here, Cap, you've gotta understand. Men have families, they just can't buckle on a gun-belt to tackle the like of these three,' protested Doc Warren.

'They had no need to get into a gunfight, I was here for that but if they'd backed me, if they'd shown strength then maybe Foster and his sidekicks would have backed down. But no, they were willing for me and Richie to become sitting targets. That's all they cared and they let poor old Mal die for a town that really wasn't worth saving.' He glared at the doctor. 'Now, you'll fix Cheyenne when I say so!' He glanced at Richie. 'Take 'em through. Cell each.'

Richie eyed the Wells brothers and motioned with his gun.

The two men turned to the door leading to the cells. As he followed them, Richie took down the key from a hook beside the door. Cap, keeping a close watch on Cheyenne, moved so that he could bring his rifle on to any of the three criminals in an instant.

Reaching the cell doors, the Wells brothers stopped. Richie motioned Joe to one side so that he could unlock the door. Joe saw that there might be a chance to seize his gun when his attention was concentrated on the lock. He cast a sharp glance in the direction of his brother who read his intention. Joe saw a warning flash from Pete's eyes and, glancing over his shoulder, he saw that Cap had been alert enough to anticipate a possible move and had them covered.

Richie unlocked the door and motioned Joe inside. Once he had locked the door on Joe, he secured Pete behind bars on the opposite side of the short corridor.

When he heard the key lock the second door, Cap turned to the doctor. 'Get on with it,' he ordered.

Doc Warren went about his task quickly and methodically and in a few minutes announced that he was finished and that, as far as he could tell, Cheyenne would be fit to travel in three days but he would see him each day to be certain. He left the office without another word, ignoring Cap's thanks. Cap took Cheyenne to the cells.

As the cell door closed behind him, Cap allowed himself to relax. 'Thanks for being around, Richie,' he said as he laid his rifle on his desk. 'Thought you'd gone out of town.'

'I had,' said the deputy, holstering his gun. 'But I got to thinking about the way things had been blowing these last two days. I figured Foster, knowing everything that happens in Pine Bluffs, would know I was going out of town and you'd be on your own; I reckoned he might try to get you. I doubled back and … well, you know the rest. Sorry I wasn't sharp enough to save Mal.' The reminder of Mal's death brought the added comment, 'Hi, Cap, you get to Laura.'

Cap glanced at the windows outside of which the crowd had grown bigger. The shouting and clamouring amongst the crowd was growing with an undercurrent of menace which Cap did not like.

'Go on,' urged Richie. 'That lot ain't got the guts to do anything, if that's why you're holding back.'

Cap gave a half laugh. 'Guess not. All the same, lock the door after me and let no one in but me.'

The two men crossed the room and, when Cap stepped outside, Richie closed and locked the door quickly.

Cap's presence on the sidewalk brought a cheer but Cap ignored it and the hero-worshipping calls which came with it.

His name was called over and over. People gave him a congratulatory slap on the back. 'Well done!' 'Nice work!' 'You showed 'em.'

Cap ignored it all, showing no sign of hearing, giving no acknowledgement of their praise as he pushed his way through the crowd. The same people who now lauded him were those who had turned their backs on him when he needed assistance. Then they had run with the outfit they thought would be victors, now they wanted to be seen and heard supporting the winner.

Once clear of the crowd Cap quickened his pace. The small group around Mal were parting and Cap saw the undertaker and his helper carrying the body towards the undertaker's workshop. Soon the ominous sound of hammer driving nails through wood would echo into the open.

Laura, dejected and forlorn, stood watching the grim procession, restrained by three women who sought to comfort and sympathise.

They nodded at Cap, when he reached the

tiny group, and discreetly left him to take over.

'Laura,' he said quietly taking her into his arms. 'I'm sorry I couldn't prevent it.'

Her eyes, in which the tears had only just dried, overflowed once more as she buried her head against his chest.

Cap let her cry, hoping it would relieve some of the desolation he knew she must be feeling from the loss of her father to whom she had been so close. He let her feel comfort from his strong arms around her, wanting her to draw strength from them to face the future in the knowledge that the world hadn't ended and that they still had their life to live together.

Her sobs subsided and she lifted her head to look up at Cap. 'Why?' she gasped. 'Why did he do it? I tried to stop him but it was no good.'

'I guess he thought if Foster escaped we had lost because Foster could come back.' Cap eased Laura out of his arms and turned her to the house. 'It was his one last act for the town he loved,' he added as they walked slowly to the house. 'An act to show the rest of the folk what they should have done. He tried to bring some self-respect back to Pine Bluffs.'

'And what's it got him?' cried Laura bitterly. 'A grave!' She paused on the veranda and looked along the street towards the crowd still milling outside the sheriff's office. 'Look at them. All for you now. Where were they when you needed them?' Her words came sharply with utter contempt. She turned to the man she was to marry. 'As soon as Pa is buried I want to go. I want to leave this town and all it means far behind me.'

'Those are my sentiments too. I've done what your pa wanted me to do. There's nothing to see to except the prisoners safely to Little Rock. Once that's done we'll go. After the way he acted today, Richie's capable of taking over.'

'Good,' said Laura. 'It can't be soon enough.' She turned to the door. 'I'll start sorting things out right away. There's no sense in moping about. Pa wouldn't want me to. Besides it will give me something to do and keep my mind occupied.'

'Good idea,' agreed Cap.

He started to follow her into the house when a sudden roar from the crowd outside his office turned him back. The noise subsided. He heard a shout and, though he could not make out the exact words, he sensed they were inflammatory. They were greeted by another roar from the crowd.

'Laura, I must go. I don't like the sound of it.'

She turned and grasped his arm. 'Be careful.' Her whisper was full of concern.

Cap patted her arm. 'I'll be back soon.' He smiled, turned and hurried off the veranda. He broke into a run as ugly yells passed through the crowd.

Nearing the edge of the gathering Cap saw that everyone's attention was so concentrated on their objective that no one had noticed his approach. He drew his Colt, raised it above his head and fired twice.

The unexpected crash brought instant silence to the milling people. Faces turned to see who had fired.

'We'll have no lynching here,' yelled Cap. Anger blazed in his eyes as he faced people who, cowards to back him, now put on a face of bravado when the gunmen were no longer a threat to them. 'Get back to your homes where you belong. Get behind the shelter of your walls which you were pleased of a few minutes ago.' He stepped forward and his attitude of contempt and menace carved him a way through the crowd. He stepped on to the sidewalk, his eyes burning with hostility at the men who stood beside the doors and windows. 'Get away from there, get down in the dust where you belong.'

Men started to shuffle off the sidewalk.

'See here, Millet…,' started a burly, bull-necked individual who held a rope in his hands.

The rest of his protest was silenced as Cap grabbed the front of the man's shirt and in the same movement yanked him forward so that he was propelled down the steps. The man would have lost his footing if it had not been for the mass of people into whom he crashed. Regaining his balance the man swung round.

'Millet, you…'

Once again Cap cut him short. 'You listen,' snapped Cap. 'You're all brave men now. Where were you when I wanted help? Mal Porter's death is on your consciences, not on Cheyenne's. He's a killer and was doing a job. You could have stopped him, but you wouldn't back me 'cos you figured Foster would win!' The contempt in Cap's voice lashed at each individual. He eyed the man with the rope. 'Drop it,' he snapped. The man let the rope slip from his fingers. 'Now get off home, all of you. Don't ever try to take the law into your own hands again, 'cos none of you are worthy of it. You ain't above the law, you're far below it.'

The crowd, muttering amongst themselves, started to disperse. A few, close to the steps, hesitated, their eyes disclosing annoyance and anger. Cap figured it was because what he had said hit at their feelings and had brought out a sense of shame, rather than because he had thwarted their rough justice through which they had sought to salve their consciences. Cap met their glares and they turned away.

Cap stood at the top of the steps, alert, his Colt ready, should any hothead still try to take matters into his own hands. He was aware that Richie had pushed open one of the office windows and held a rifle.

When the crowd had dispersed to his satisfaction, Cap holstered his gun and turned to the office. Richie cast one more glance along the street, closed the window and unlocked the door.

'Glad you came back,' said Richie. 'Thanks.'

'You'd have held them,' replied Cap.

'I'd have tried but they were getting a bit ugly. Guess I should have got outside and quelled it before it started.'

'There's always a lesson to be learned,'

smiled Cap.

'Sure. And I've got a good teacher,' said Richie.

'Not got, son, had,' said Cap.

For a moment the words did not register and then the implication behind them drew a gasp from the young deputy. 'You quitting?'

'Not quitting, leaving,' answered Cap. 'You knew Laura and I were set on a ranch up north.'

'Sure, but I didn't expect you'd be leaving so soon, not for a year or two.'

'Well it might have worked out that way but after what has happened there's nothing to hold us here. Pine Bluffs will only have bad memories for Laura even though she has had happy times here, so the sooner we leave the better.'

'But what about the job? What about the law?'

'I'm looking at it,' grinned Cap.

'Me? Sheriff?' Richie stared at Cap in disbelief.

Three

'Cap, we don't like it.'

Cap fixed Jim Maltby with an unflinching stare as the other four men grouped behind the town mayor murmured their agreement.

'You'll have to get used to it because I'm leaving. I reckon you've thought it over and can't come up with anyone else to take my job.'

Jim moved his big frame uncomfortably. He had not looked forward to this interview since getting Cap's note handing in his resignation and advising him to back Richie for sheriff. Jim had called an immediate meeting of the town council and, as much as it went against their pride, they realised that they must approach Cap.

'Look, I know how it looked, I know how you felt when no one backed you…'

51

'You couldn't know,' broke in Cap sharply. 'You weren't me. And don't ever say no one backed me, Richie did, Laura did, and remember Mal? He did, with his life.'

The five men diverted their eyes from Cap as his glance threw accusations at each one in turn.

'All right, Cap, we know it looked bad, but you must remember how folks felt at that particular time.'

'Sure, I remember. Gutless. Different story as soon as I had them *hombres* behind bars. Brave men came forward, keen to know me, keen then to throw their weight about and head for lynching helpless men.' Cap's eyes conveyed the disgust in his voice.

'All right, all right,' blustered Jim, 'let's forget the past, it's the future we're thinking about.'

'That ain't difficult,' said Cap. 'Appoint Richie as sheriff.' He leaned back in his chair and let his gaze run over the deputation. 'You know, I reckon I've felt a change in atmosphere since the shooting two days ago. I figure there's some spunk back in this town. Men hold their heads up again. They've got some pride in their town once more. Maybe now they'd act differently.'

'Sure we would,' put in Jim quickly, eager to seize a chance to exonerate himself. The other four men brightened visibly and backed the mayor with their assertive agreements. 'We'll back you any way you want, if you'll stay on as sheriff.'

Cap shook his head slowly. 'Not a chance.'

'Rise in pay, after what you did.'

'Give it to Richie, he played his part, out-manoeuvred the Cheyenne Kid when I was in a difficult position, remember?'

'Ain't he a bit young?' put in the small, thin man who ran the town's newspaper. His hands fiddled nervously with his black hat.

'He conducted himself a mite better than a lot of older men in this town. You want the job, Brooks?'

The newspaperman shuffled with embarrassment. 'No, no. I didn't mean that I … I…' His words faded away as he was unable to explain his attitude.

'Millet, er … Cap,' Jim blustered in. 'I hear you're heading north, figuring on taking up ranching.' Jim hesitated, half-waiting for confirmation. When it didn't come he went on. 'If that's so, I reckon we can fix you up here, you could have your ranch and combine it with the sheriff's job.'

The mayor's companions nodded their assent.

Cap glanced at them all before making his reply. They had it all cut and dried, offer him anything to keep him in Pine Bluffs. They were still frightened.

Cap shook his head slowly. 'No. Can't do two jobs.'

'You'd have Richie here in town,' pressed Jim. 'No need for you to be away from your ranch.'

Cap cast the mayor a look of contempt. 'You just want me as a gunman in case you need one.'

'No, no,' protested Jim quickly, looking hurt that Cap should think such a thing, but the colouring of his face gave him away.

'Sure you do,' rapped Cap. 'Oh, no, I'm not playing with that idea. I'm leaving.'

'Consider, Laura,' put in Brooks. 'She's spent most of her life here. She…'

'That's just what I am doing,' cut in Cap harshly. 'She wants to get away as soon as possible. This place will have a bad memory for her. And you folks will too. You let her father get killed, remember?'

'See here, Millet,' Brooks raised a spark of protest. 'The Cheyenne Kid killed him, not us.'

The other townsfolk backed him with murmured objections.

'You allowed the Cheyenne Kid to exist here. If you'd had any spunk at all you'd have backed what Mal was trying to do and the situation of a shoot-out wouldn't have arisen.'

'Cap, Foster got away,' Jim pointed out wanting to leave Mal's killing and try a new tack to get Cap to stay. 'He could come back.'

'I don't figure he will,' replied Cap. 'He

needs gunmen and they'll be in the Pen for a long time.'

'But…'

'That's the end of the matter,' put in Cap. 'I'm leaving, and that's my final word. Richie's capable of looking after your precious town. I have things to see to, gentlemen, so I'd be obliged if you'd leave.'

He ignored their looks of annoyance as they shuffled out of his office. Only the mayor showed any bluster as he pushed past the others.

Cap leaned back in his chair with a sigh. He hoped the doctor would pass Cheyenne fit to travel when he made his examination later in the day. He and Laura wanted to shake the dust of Pine Bluffs off their feet.

She had busied herself packing and disposing of unwanted items, working with an eager zest to keep her mind off her father's death and to have everything ready as soon as possible. Cap had been surprised at the speed with which she had gone about things and he knew at this very moment, with the help of a couple of youngsters, she was packing the wagon he had purchased.

The door opened and Richie came in. 'Waited until I saw that deputation leave, guessed it was you they wanted to see.'

Cap grinned wryly. 'Sure was. Tried to get me to stay.'

'And?' prompted Richie.

'I ain't. The job's yours as far as I'm concerned. I figure Jim Maltby'll be seeing you.'

'I'll be sorry to see you go.'

'Thanks,' smiled Cap. He noted a touch of apprehension in Richie's eyes. He stood up and moved round his desk. 'You'll be all right, you'll do a good job,' Cap reassured him as he slapped him on the shoulder. 'I'll start handing over to you now. Then, if the doc passes Cheyenne fit, we'll take the prisoners to Little Rock tomorrow. Stay the night there, back the next day and the day after it's goodbye Pine Bluffs.'

The handing-over procedure went smoothly and Cap offered some advice. 'Keep the right side of Kate Robson, she can be a good ally as she's already proved. And she knows most of what goes on around here.'

Before Richie could voice his agreement the door opened and the doctor walked in. He gave the two lawmen a cursory nod and followed Richie to the cells. When they came out again the doctor paused and said, 'Cheyenne can move.'

'Thanks,' said Cap, but Doc Warren, ignoring Cap's response, was already half-way to the door.

'Ornery old cuss,' said Cap, staring at the closed door. 'Never really liked my coming here. Could never put my finger on why.'

'I've no reason for saying this but I figure he was in on some of Foster's deals,' said Richie.

Cap eyed his deputy. 'No proof?'

Richie shook his head. 'None. Just a feeling. I saw the doc and Foster together several times. Mostly in the Golden Cage having a drink.'

'Nothing unusual in that,' said Cap. 'Doc

Warren likes his drink but that's his affair. I never heard of him slipping up on a case because of it.'

'That's right,' agreed Richie. 'I talked to Kate about him but she knew no more than I did.'

'If there was anything between Foster and the doc, I reckon Kate would know.'

'That's what I figured, but the doc's a wily bird.'

'Sure. You watch out for him if you have any suspicions,' advised Cap. He shrugged his shoulders. 'But maybe he just didn't like me. Well, he's approved us moving Cheyenne so we'll do it tomorrow.'

When Cap arrived at the sheriff's office the following morning he found that Richie was already supervising the arrival of the stableman with the prisoner's horses.

Word had got round Pine Bluffs that Cap and Richie were leaving with the gunmen and a small crowd was gathering around the office while other people waited on the side-walks.

'Ghoulish lot,' muttered Cap as he strode into the office. 'What pleasure do they get from seeing the likes of the Wells brothers and Cheyenne being taken for trial?' The disgust in his voice summed up his opinion of most of the folks in Pine Bluffs. 'Right, Richie, let's have 'em out, one at a time.'

The deputy took down the bunch of keys from the hook on the wall and preceded Cap to the cells.

'Fancy a ride to Little Rock?' called Cap.

'Not really, we're comfortable here,' replied Joe sarcastically without moving from the bed on which he was lying.

'Sure are,' agreed his brother with a grin.

'Well, you're riding whether you like it or not,' snapped Cap. 'On your feet. You first, Joe.'

Richie moved to the cell door and un-locked it. Joe did not move. Cap stepped into the cell. 'Move!' he rapped. Joe smiled. Cap stepped towards him. Joe swung off the bed and in the same quick, lithe movement was on his feet.

Cap was almost taken by surprise but his reaction came with lightning swiftness. He had Joe covered with his Colt.

Joe stretched and grinned. He eyed the Colt and then met Cap's smouldering eyes. 'You jumpy, Sheriff?' His smile broadened. 'Figuring this ain't going to be an easy ride?' He chuckled as he stepped past Cap. Cap swung round and followed him.

'Pete next,' Cap said tersely.

Richie waited a few moments for Cap to settle his prisoner outside before he unlocked Pete's cell. The gunslinger did not speak but merely grinned at Richie, giving him the uncomfortable feeling that the gunmen were up to something. He escorted Pete outside where Joe was already on his horse which was still tethered to the hitching rail.

Cap nodded. 'Now, Cheyenne.' As Richie turned back into the office, Cap motioned to Pete to get on to his horse.

Comments were buzzing through the crowd, surprised that up to now Cap had made no move to secure the prisoners. Their attentions changed when the Cheyenne Kid appeared. He limped across the sidewalk, eased himself down the steps and moved to the side of his horse.

'Hi, Collins, you'll have to help me, this leg you damaged...' Cheyenne called over his shoulder.

Richie hesitated a moment, then holstered his gun and stepped to the prisoner. 'Right, put your good leg in the...'

In that instant the Kid brought his right arm swiftly downwards, sending his elbow hard into the stomach of the man who stood behind him.

Richie doubled up sharply as his words choked on the air which was driven from his lungs. He staggered backwards, grasping at the hurt which seared from his stomach.

The moment he made contact, Cheyenne swung smoothly upwards into the saddle and when Richie looked up with venom in his eyes he saw the Kid grinning at him. 'Just something to remember me by and to remind you that one day I'll be coming after you.'

'Stow it, Kid!' Cap's voice rapped harshly above the heightened murmuring coming from the crowd. His Colt menaced the prisoner.

'Going to shoot me now, Lawman? Just so's I can't get your wet-behind-the-ears deputy?' There was derision and contempt in Cheyenne's voice.

Richie, still writhing from the blow, tensed himself at the taunt. He straightened and started towards the Kid.

'Cool it, Richie!' rapped Cap. Another time, another place and he might have allowed the youngster to show the Kid just how wrong he was in his judgement. But now Cap's main concern was to get the prisoners safely to Little Rock.

Cap's words brought Richie to a halt. The deputy swung round and glared at Cap. The older man met Richie's unspoken protests with a look which withered any thought of retaliation on Cheyenne.

Fuming, Richie grabbed his stetson from

the ground and slapped the dust from it.

'Lock the office, Richie,' said Cap firmly.

Once this had been done, the deputy went to his horse and swung into the saddle.

'Keep 'em covered,' Cap ordered. 'If any of them show the least sign of trying to escape shoot 'em.' His words were meant as much as a deadly warning to his prisoners as an instruction to Richie.

When Cap saw that Richie was settled in the saddle and had drawn his Colt, he holstered his gun and moved to the hitching rail.

'Hi, Lawman, ain't you tying us?' There was a note of mockery in Joe's voice.

Cap stopped and eyed the man on the horse. 'We'll make better time if you're loose,' said Cap. His voice went cold. 'But don't get any ideas about escaping. There's two of us with guns ready to drop you on the slightest suspicion. I ain't worried if you don't make Little Rock to stand before a judge.'

'You threatening?' put in Pete.

'No, warning!' rapped Cap. He turned to the hitching rail putting an end to any more exchanges. He was satisfied that the gunmen knew their position perfectly. He swung smoothly into the saddle, turned the animal and motioned to the prisoners to move off.

The three men backed their mounts away from the rail and turned them to leave Pine Bluffs in the direction of Little Rock. The lawmen positioned themselves behind them and the crowd parted to allow them to pass.

Cap was not oblivious to the comments which were thrown in the direction of the riders and he noted with some disquiet that a few were in sympathy with the prisoners.

The murmurings gradually ceased as the group rode at a walking pace along the main street. People lining both sidewalks watched the riders pass in silence.

As they approached Laura's house, Cap saw that she was standing beside the wagon, partially loaded for coming departure. His glance at Richie was answered by a slight nod of understanding – extra vigilance while

Cap's attention was diverted from the prisoners.

Cap momentarily halted his horse when he reached Laura. 'Be back tomorrow, love,' he said quietly with a reassuring smile.

'Take care,' she whispered in return, with her eyes reflecting the dread and worry she felt inside her.

'I will.' Cap pursed his lips in a kiss and tapped his horse into a trot to catch up with Richie and the prisoners.

Once clear of the town, Cap ordered a quickening of pace.

They made good progress as Cap ignored the oft-repeated calls from one gunman or another for a halt. He was determined to let nothing stop them reaching Little Rock before nightfall.

At noon he called a halt beside a tree-lined stream. 'One hour,' he said. 'Rest the horses, water them and get some grub.' He eyed the three men still in the saddles. 'Easy, we'll do this one at a time. Richie tie the horses to that branch.' Richie holstered his gun to carry out

Cap's instructions. Cap immediately felt a tension come to the prisoners and he guessed they were contemplating some action with only one gun trained on them.

'Forget it,' he rapped. 'I can blow one of you out of the saddle almost before you move, but which one? Anyone willing to take a chance to find out?'

The gunmen eyed each other, each wondering if either of the others would take that chance. Joe quickly flashed a warning to his brother and Cheyenne.

'Sensible,' commented Cap as he felt the tension disappear. 'Right, Richie,' he went on, when the deputy had secured the horses. 'You'll find three pieces of rope in my saddlebag, tie their feet when they are sitting on the ground. You first, Joe.'

The gunman hesitated fractionally but he saw nothing to be gained by not complying with Cap's order. He swung from the saddle and sat in a spot indicated by Richie who had the ropes in his hand. Careful not to get between the prisoner and Cap's gun, Richie quickly secured Joe's feet. He went through the same procedure with the other two prisoners, placing them sufficiently apart so that they had no physical contact.

'Right, Richie, give them something to eat.'

An hour later, with everyone fed, the horses watered and rested, Cap adopted the same precautionary measures to get them on the trail again.

As they moved on, Joe called over his shoulder, 'Millet, what's it take for you and your deputy to let us go?' The gunman, realising that Cap's vigilance was not going to relax, was prepared to try anything to escape a stretch in the Pen.

Cap ignored the query.

'You hear me, Millet?' asked Joe.

Joe suddenly halted his horse. For one brief moment he thought he had broken the vigilance but then realised that Cap's Colt had not wavered.

'What'll buy you off?' Joe shot quickly.

'Keep moving,' rapped Cap, ignoring the query.

Joe sent his horse forward again in a brooding silence.

'Hi, Deputy, what about you?' It was Pete's turn to try to undermine the law.

Richie rode on without a word.

'He's too chicken-livered to throw in with us,' commented Cheyenne, with a touch of derision in his voice. Maybe they could needle Collins into retaliation which would bring confusion and give them a chance to escape.

Joe realised what the Kid was trying to do and took up the baiting. 'We wouldn't want him, Kid, not when he fell so easily for that trick of yours back in Pine Bluffs.'

'He was a right sucker!' laughed Pete.

'Saw the way he doubled up,' added Joe.

Kid laughed loudly. 'And in front of all those townsfolk, the man who's going to be their next sheriff!'

'Falling for an old trick like that,' roared Joe.

Cap stiffened. He saw Richie weakening under the taunts, saw his temper boiling to the surface. If that exploded all hell could be let loose. Cap edged his horse nearer to the deputy. 'Steady, Richie.' His whisper held an urgency for obedience. 'Quit it you three,' he called, raising his voice. 'Richie ain't going to fall for your tricks.'

Richie closed his eyes and shook his head as if ridding himself of the words which pounded tauntingly in his mind. He took a deep breath, opened his eyes and glanced at Cap. 'I'm all right,' he said.

Silence fell over the group once again. Cap settled the riders into a pace he knew would enable them to reach Little Rock before nightfall. With the town in sight, Cap half-expected that the gunmen might throw all caution aside and try something desperate, but they sensed his extra vigilance and remained passive.

The group of riders brought a few curious glances as they rode along Main Street to the sheriff's office.

'Watch 'em Richie,' Cap called and swung to the ground. He stepped on to the sidewalk and entered the office. 'Dutch Harper?' he asked.

The lawman eyed the newcomer from behind his desk. 'That's me,' he drawled casually.

'Cap Millet from Pine Bluffs,' said Cap. 'Brought the three prisoners I contacted you about.'

'Right. Let's get 'em behind bars,' said the big, broad-shouldered sheriff of Little Rock, pushing himself to his feet. There was no offered hand of welcome or easing of the disinterested expression on his face. This was strictly business and that's the way it was going to stay.

Cap made no comment. If that was how Harper wanted it then so be it.

The two men went out on to the sidewalk and under their vigilant eyes the three gunmen were brought through the office to the cells. Once they were locked in separate cells, the lawmen returned to the office where Cap introduced his deputy to Dutch.

'I fixed for the Circuit judge to be here day

71

after tomorrow,' said Dutch.

'Who?' asked Cap.

'Judge Wilson.'

'Don't know him.'

'Has a reputation for being a bit easy-going,' said Dutch.

'You want no easy-going judge for the *hombres* you got in there.'

Dutch shrugged his shoulders. 'Well, that's Judge Wilson.'

'Maybe it would help if I stick around for the trial,' said Cap.

'Dunno about that,' replied Dutch. 'We've got sufficient on the prisoners to put 'em away for a long time. No need for you to hang around.'

'Maybe, my evidence of events in Pine Bluffs would put 'em away for longer.'

'You never can tell with Judge Wilson. There's no need for you to stay but if you want to…'

Cap was curious. He was surprised that Dutch didn't readily accept his offer. It seemed as if the troubles in Pine Bluffs were unimportant and would be overlooked if he was not at the trial.

'Richie, I'm going to stay,' Cap said suddenly. 'You return as planned and tell Laura what's happened. I hope she'll understand.'

Four

'Want me to help with the prisoners?' Cap put the question as he walked into Dutch's office two days later.

'Thanks,' replied Dutch, 'but my deputies will see they reach the court.'

Cap nodded. He felt snubbed. But he realised he was on another lawman's territory and, like many others, Dutch wanted no one else butting in. Cap left the office and walked slowly to the saloon which had been closed for the morning so that it could act as a court room.

A number of townsfolk were already converging on the building and Cap knew that, before the trial got underway, the room would be full. No one took any notice of him as he strolled into the saloon and found himself a seat on the front row.

Twenty minutes later a small, slightly built man dressed in a black frock-coat and matching trousers followed the broad-framed Dutch who made a way through the throng of people standing between the chairs and the bar counter. Reaching the table which had been set at one end of the room, the man put down the sheaf of papers he was carrying. He took off his low-crowned, black hat and glanced over the tin-rimmed spectacles perched on the end of his nose. Dutch said something quietly to him and received a nod in reply.

Dutch took out his Colt and rapped the butt hard on the table. The noise in the room subsided.

'Judge Wilson's court is now in session.' Dutch called so that he could be heard in every corner of the room.

The judge sat down, glanced at his papers and then looked at the crowded room. 'There are six cases to be heard here,' he said. 'I don't intend to dally over them, I have other important things to see to.'

'Like the red-head in Cool Springs!' The shout from someone at the back of the room brought loud laughter and more comment from the rest of the spectators.

The judge seemed to shrink at the remark. He cast a sharp glance at Dutch, who jumped to his feet and pounded on the table with the butt of his gun.

'Quiet! Quiet!' he yelled. 'Let's have some respect for the judge.'

The small man shuffled uneasily in his chair and when he looked up his eyes were burning with annoyance. 'Any more trouble and the room will be cleared.' His thin voice penetrated the last subsiding remarks.

Cap had studied the man with interest. The thin, gaunt face did nothing to inspire confidence. The tone in his words only added to Cap's disapproval, and Cap wondered how the judge would handle the hardened gunmen who were to be brought before him.

The first two cases brought more shouted comments and the judge showed no sign of carrying out his threat to clear the room.

Cap realised that the townsfolk knew they could get away with anything and that the day this circuit judge came were days when they could take liberties and generally have a good laugh at his expense. He was a far cry from most of the judges Cap had come across. The hilarity continued and showed approval of the light sentences passed on the men on trial.

When Dutch called for the Wells brothers and the Cheyenne Kid to be brought before the judge the noise in the saloon sank quickly to hushed whispers. A few moments later Dutch's deputies escorted the gunmen to the area marked out for prisoners at one side of the judge's table.

The judge looked up from some papers he had been studying when the gunmen were brought in. He eyed them over the top of his spectacles.

'Joe Wells, Pete Wells, Cheyenne Kid, it says here that you are wanted for rape and murder in Jackson County. How plead you?'

'It ain't right, Judge,' answered Joe.

Pete and the Kid gave weight to Joe's reply. 'Straight up, Judge. We did nothing.'

The judge grunted. 'The woman says…'

'Hi, hold it, Judge,' Joe interrupted. 'You can't try us on the written word. Is the woman we're supposed to have raped here to testify?'

The judge glared at Joe for interrupting but did not reprimand him. Instead he looked at the sheriff. 'Is she here?' he asked.

Dutch shook his head. 'No.'

The judge looked exasperated.

'Read it out, Judge,' someone yelled from the back of the crowd. 'We'd like to hear how they did it.'

The request brought a loud roar of anticipation from the rest of the people in the saloon.

The sheriff banged on the table.

As the noise subsided, Joe put in quickly, 'If she ain't here to tell her story you can't believe what's written down, Judge.'

Judge Wilson made no comment, instead he said, 'Now the murder is a different thing. Says here that you shot two men.'

'Judge, we never did, not so's you could call it murder.' Joe put on an innocent look. He turned to his brother and Cheyenne. 'Ain't that right?'

'Sure is,' they agreed.

A faint smile flicked the corners of the judge's mouth. 'Ah, but it says here that there were witnesses.'

'What, witnesses again? Here?' grinned Pete, expecting Joe to back him with a demand for someone to come forward and testify.

But before Joe could do so the judge said, 'Yes, one of them's here.'

A buzz went round the saloon. The Wells brothers and the Cheyenne Kid had a reputation which was well known but no one had ever been able to prove anything against them and whenever they had been brought before a judge there was never anyone who would come forward to testify.

The prisoners, surprised by the judge's statement, glanced sharply at each other.

'It says here,' the judge went on, 'that two years ago five of you held up the bank in Pincher Creek.'

'Right, Judge, we won't deny that, but that ain't murder.' Joe's admission of robbing the bank surprised Pete until he realised that Joe was playing the judge along. 'Hardly a robbery either, the bank lost no money, they got it all back.'

'That's right,' agreed the judge. 'That's what it says here, but it also says that you three were responsible for the deaths of your two partners.'

'How?' Joe feigned his surprise so well that everyone in the room thought it was genuine. 'What sort of folks does that make us?'

'Murderers,' replied the judge as if he did not like to make the direct accusation. 'And as I said there is a witness here.'

Joe, Pete and the Cheyenne Kid looked round the room.

'Who?' asked the Kid. 'Who's going to testify against us?' he added, addressing his question to the crowd with a menace in his voice which brooked no good if anyone dared to speak.

A hum of comment and question rose from the crowd as neighbours eyed each other wondering if they were looking at the witness.

'This report tells me that you were recognised by a couple of the citizens of Pincher Creek as you went into the bank and, figuring you were up to no good, they called the law quickly, so that by the time you came out there were people armed to stop you.' The judge paused and glanced over his spectacles at the prisoners. Joe nodded. The judge looked at his papers again and continued: 'It says that during the exchanges of fire you took the opportunity to kill your partners, who were carrying the money, so's you'd have a bigger share, but the gunfire was so intense that you couldn't get to it.'

Joe let out a low whistle and rolled his eyes upwards. 'Some folks have real imaginations!'

'You deny it?' asked the judge.

'Of course, because it didn't happen.'

'But it says there was a witness.'

'So you keep saying, but you ain't naming,' snapped Cheyenne.

'Says here,' said the judge tapping the paper, 'that Sheriff Dutch Harper was serving as a deputy in Pincher Creek at the time.'

The unexpected information brought a new wave of noise rippling through the room. Dutch, startled by the judge's words, straightened in his chair. His eyes widened with surprise. This was the last thing he had expected to hear or even wanted to hear. He shot a glance at the prisoners.

'How say you, Dutch? Were you serving in Pincher Creek at the time of this hold-up?' asked the judge.

'Er … yes,' answered Dutch.

'Then let's hear your version of what happened.'

Dutch's mind had been racing back to that time in Pincher Creek, in fact more precisely to the time after the raid. The three men standing trial now were certainly involved, he could not deny that but as to murder ... well, he was certain that he had made no statement at the time.

'Sure, five men held up the bank, two were killed and three escaped.'

'Are the three prisoners those who escaped?' asked the judge.

'Yes,' replied Dutch weakly.

'Did you see who killed the other two?'

'No. Everyone was firing.'

'Then you couldn't testify that they deliberately shot their accomplices?'

'Hell, no, Judge,' replied Dutch, feeling more confident. 'Who could say, with so much lead flying around?'

The judge nodded. 'Were any of the citizens of Pincher Creek killed?'

'No.'

'Was all the money recovered?'

'Yes. The two robbers who died were carrying the cash. When they were shot, Joe Wells tried to get to it but the fire from the townsfolk was so intense that even the covering fire from his brother and Cheyenne couldn't help him and he had to leave it.'

'Mm.' The judge pondered thoughtfully for a moment. 'So, no one was killed, except for the two robbers; the money was recovered… That right?'

'Sure, sure,' answered Dutch hastily as if he wanted to get the matter out of the way.

The judge fished his pocket watch from his waistcoat, glanced at it and replaced it.

'In that case the prisoners have no murder charge to answer, the money was recovered so they can't be tried for robbery so all I can sentence them for is a breach of the peace.' He paused then added, 'Two years!'

Pandemonium broke out.

Cap was thunderstruck by the lightness of the sentence and by what he had witnessed. The trial had been a mockery of justice. The troubles at Pine Bluffs had never been raised. Seeing the relief in Dutch's eyes, he felt sure that the sheriff of Little Rock was walking close to the edge of the law in his relationship with the prisoners.

Cap jumped to his feet. 'Judge! Judge!' he

yelled. 'These men are known killers, they deserve to be put away for a long time!'

Cap's words pierced the noise and as people realised what had been said they began to quieten. Eyes turned to see who challenged the judge's decision.

'Who the hell are you?' snapped the judge, irritated by the fact that his departure was being delayed.

'Cap Millet, present Sheriff of Pine Bluffs.'

'And what the hell have you got to do with this?'

'I brought these prisoners in. I had trouble with them in Pine Bluffs. They were guns hired by a man called Foster who was ruling the town with the help of their muscle.'

'So? What's that to do with this trial?'

'Their whole reputations should be taken into account and any other crimes they've committed…'

'I ain't here to have a run-down on their whole life and pass judgment on that. I'm here to try these men for the crimes indi-

86

cated in my papers and it says nothing about any happenings in Pine Bluffs. The charges have been pending for some time and when Sheriff Harper informed me they were being brought into Little Rock then I figured these were the crimes they were to be charged with.'

'But this is...'

'That's the end of the matter.'

'Judge you can't...'

'I can and I have.' The judge stood up. 'And if I have any more from you I'll have Sheriff Harper arrest you for contempt.'

Cap stared dumbfounded by the judge's attitude. 'The Cheyenne Kid killed a man in Pine Bluffs!' he called.

'That ain't in my papers!' rapped the judge. He turned to the sheriff. 'Get him out of here.'

Dutch needed no second bidding. Cap Millet could cause trouble and he wanted none of that. The trial had gone well. Two years was nothing. He'd get his cut in due course for playing things down.

He moved his big frame quickly across the room, drawing his Colt as he did so. 'Come on, Millet, let's have no trouble. I don't want the judge to order me to arrest you. Leave quietly.'

Cap bit back the retort which sprang to his lips. He too wanted no trouble. If he bucked the judge again he could wind up in gaol and he didn't want that. He wanted to be back in Pine Bluffs, with Laura and on their way to Montana. If he'd known that the trial was going to turn out like this he would have remained with Richie. His stay had been of no avail. Cap was disgusted. The whole trial had been a farce and, though he realised he would never be able to prove it, he felt sure that somewhere along the line Dutch and possibly the judge were running with the prisoners. He shrugged his shoulders resignedly. What the hell did it matter? To push the killing of Mal Porter now would only cause more trouble and more heartache and pain for Laura. It wouldn't bring her father back and it would delay the departure for Montana on which Laura had set her heart.

Cap glared at the sheriff and turned to leave the saloon, but he was pulled up short by a shout from Pete Wells. 'So long, Millet. Went to a lot of trouble for nothing, didn't yer?' The mocking tones jabbed hard at Cap. It took him all his time to keep his temper. He started for the door with the contemptuous laughter of the three prisoners pounding at his mind. All eyes watched him and murmurings rippled through the crowd as he made no response but walked to the door instead.

Once outside on the sidewalk, Cap stopped and turned to Dutch. 'You can put that away,' he said indicating the lawman's Colt. 'I ain't going to pull anything on you. You just ain't worth it. How much are you in with those three coyotes?'

Annoyance darkened Dutch's face. 'I'm not.' His voice showed such irritation that Cap knew there was something between the lawman and the prisoners. 'Look, Millet, this is my territory and you count for nothing on it. I'm the law here and I uphold the judge whichever way his decisions go. Now, I figure if you don't play that way you ain't got any business being a lawman.'

'Ain't how I see the job, but what the hell? I've had my taste of sheriffing and I'm quitting it for ranching. I did the job I came to Pine Bluffs to do. What do I get? The likes of you and that weak-kneed judge fouling my efforts.' Cap's voice showed his disgust and contempt. 'Only one thing, Pine Bluffs has got rid of them.'

Dutch glared at Cap. 'Take my advice and quit town now. If you buck me again I won't be answerable for the consequences.'

'You needn't worry,' snapped Cap. 'I'm leaving. The sooner I get rid of the stench of this town the better.' He swung round and hurried in the direction of the livery stables.

Half an hour later Cap had put the town behind him and he did not look back.

He knew he would not reach Pine Bluffs that night but if he camped on the trail he would reach the town the next morning and then he and Laura could leave just as soon as she wished.

Laura was delighted to see Cap swinging from the saddle just before noon the next day. She hurried out to greet him.

'I hope your stay was worthwhile,' she said after they had exchanged kisses and were walking arm in arm to the house.

'It damn well wasn't,' replied Cap and went on to tell her what had happened in Little Rock.

'So it was all wrong,' said Laura. 'And Pa's killer will be out of gaol in a couple of years, there isn't any justice.' She steeled herself against the tears which threatened to flow.

'When do you want to leave?' asked Cap.

'The sooner the better. But you'll have to see Richie and there are a few things left to pack. I'll get on with those now then we can be away first thing in the morning.'

'Fine,' agreed Cap.

Twenty minutes later Cap took his horse to the livery stable where he instructed the stableman to take care of it and to have it ready together with two other horses and the team of four for the wagon early the following morning.

Cap left the livery stable and hurried to the sheriff's office where Richie was soon in possession of the happenings in Little Rock.

'So in two years those bastards could be back here again.' There was concern in Richie's voice.

'I don't figure so,' said Cap. 'I reckon they'll figure you have the townsfolk behind you now, besides they won't operate without someone to organise them and I can't see Foster coming back here now.'

Before Richie could reply, the door opened and the doctor walked in. He offered no greeting but asked, 'Cheyenne have any ill effects, wasn't sure if I sent him too soon?'

'He was all right,' replied Cap.

'So what did they get?' asked the doctor.

'Two years.'

'Two years! Is that all?' Cap couldn't be sure whether the doctor's surprise was really genuine with disgust or not.

'Yeah. The judge should be drummed off the circuit.'

'Two years,' mused the doctor. 'And with remission for good behaviour that could mean eighteen months at the most.'

'Yes.'

The doctor made no more comment but turned on his heel and left the office without a word of goodbye.

'Queer old cuss,' said Richie when the door closed.

'I'm not sure I'd trust him,' said Cap. 'You'd be smart if you kept tabs on him.'

'I'll do that,' said Richie. 'You don't figure he's in cahoots with those gun-slingers?'

'Not directly, only in so far as he's in with Foster.'

'But he's gone. And as you say not likely to come back, so what can the doc get up to?'

'Don't know, but it's a good idea to keep your eye on anyone who makes you feel uneasy.' Cap was tempted to tell Richie that the railway might be coming to Pine Bluffs but he figured it better not to. He had been trusted with a secret and passing the information to Richie would serve no purpose, especially as he reckoned Foster was unlikely to return.

He would not have felt as easy had he known that, at the same time as he was making this decision, Doc Warren was arranging to be out of town for four days.

Five

When Doc Warren rode into Lonesome two days later he was glad to see the saloon. He was not one for the outdoors and preferred the comparative comfort of a wooden chair beside a wooden table than to taking his drink under the open sky.

His bottle of whisky had provided some counter to the discomforts of sleeping on the ground and he did not look forward to the night he would have to spend in the open on his return journey to Pine Bluffs.

All he hoped was that it would be worthwhile. If old man Porter hadn't let his pride for his town rule him the suffering of the past two days wouldn't have been necessary. Bringing Cap Millet in had ruined everything, but now he figured there was a slim chance that he might be able to salvage something from the upheaval.

The doc thought Lonesome fitted its name just right. It looked neglected and forgotten. Buildings were falling into disrepair and, though there were people on the sidewalks, Doc Warren saw that they were not the usual run of townsfolk.

He licked his lips nervously when he felt hostile eyes on him. The men in his view were rough, hard cases and the few women who talked to them were obviously hangers-on, there to provide a service for what money they could get and the hope that one day the man they fancied would hit it rich and whisk them away to a life of luxury.

Lonesome and its folk looked exactly what it had become, a ghost town which had seen better days before it was abandoned to be eventually used by the lawless as a hideout between 'jobs'. It had a reputation which kept lawmen away and, as he rode towards the saloon, Doc Warren knew why.

The suspicion and hostility which was emanating from the folk on the sidewalk could easily turn to bullets if the stranger showed the slightest hint of riding with the law on his side.

Doc Warren eased himself slowly from the saddle and swung gently to the ground. His face wrinkled with annoyance and some pain as he stretched his aching limbs. He muttered under his breath and stomped up the three steps on to the sidewalk.

The batwings squeaked as he pushed them open and left them swinging behind him as he walked into the saloon.

The room had had little care and attention devoted to it since Lonesome's relegation from a decent town. It had been maintained to a level of use which satisfied the type of customers it now catered for.

A burly, thick-necked individual eyed Doc Warren as the doc came to the long counter.

'Whisky,' said the doc.

The dark growth around the barman's chin made him look more untidy than he really was. He nodded at Doc Warren's order and turned to reach for a bottle and glass on the shelf behind him.

Doc noted the huge hands which placed them on the counter in front of him. Their size seemed to warn customers that he would stand no nonsense in a saloon which he was running for their benefit. Doc felt sure that even the most hardened cases would avoid antagonising this man.

'Stranger here.' The barman's words were clipped and to the point and demanded an explanation even though they were not put as a question.

'Yeah,' replied the doc. 'And mighty glad to get out of the saddle.'

'Ain't used to riding, I'd say,' commented the barman, noting Doc's wriggling to ease the discomfort he was feeling.

'Sure ain't. You can keep your damned horse as a means of transport except when pulling a buggy.' The doc tipped his glass to his mouth, drained its contents and poured another. He smacked his lips. 'That's better.'

'Why you here? Lonesome doesn't generally attract the likes of you. And if you've ridden here when you don't like horses you must have had some good reason.'

Doc realised he had been scrutinised and now had to give a good account of himself or he wouldn't leave this town alive. 'I'm looking for someone,' he said and realised immediately that he had put this man on his guard.

The barman's eyes narrowed. 'You some kind of lawman?'

'Hell, no.' The doc drained his glass again and refilled it. 'You figure I'd be here if I were?'

'Well, you don't look like one,' admitted the barman, his tone lightening. 'So who are you? You pack no gun, yet you ride in here...'

'Doc Warren's the name,' interrupted the doctor. 'I'm looking for a fellah from Pine Bluffs, Clay Foster. Probably rode in here about a week ago.'

'Riding a big chestnut?'

'That'd be him.'

'You'll find him in the hotel, if that's what

you like to call it. There's some who'd give it a different name.'

'Thanks.' The doc drank once more, looked at the bottle again. He was tempted to have another but decided against it. 'Guess I'll look him up.' He paid for his drinks and turned away from the bar.

He paused on the sidewalk and located the hotel sign hanging in a drunken posture from one hook. Leaving his horse where it was he walked steadily to the hotel. When he entered the building he found that, like the saloon, the upkeep had been just sufficient to enable it to maintain its rating as a hotel.

A small man with a pointed nose, below which a moustache separated it from a thin-lipped mouth, stood behind a desk, with his arm round a girl whom the doc reckoned was young enough to be his granddaughter.

'Looking for a man named Clay Foster,' said Doc Warren, aware that he was coming under the curious scrutiny of the girl whom he figured was probably viewing him as a potential customer.

'Room fourteen.' The thin man hardly gave Doc any attention.

As he walked up the stairs he glanced back to the lobby and saw that the couple were no longer concerned about him. He went to the second floor and found the room he was looking for.

He knocked on the door. He heard a scuffling inside the room and the patter of feet approach the door. It was eased open slowly until someone was able to see out.

Doc saw he was being scrutinised by a girl. 'What do you want?' she asked, her voice surly.

'Clay Foster.'

'He's busy, go away.' The girl started to close the door but Doc stuck his foot in the way.

'Foster,' he called out, 'Doc Warren here.'

He heard some muttering and then a voice he recognised as Foster's said, 'Let him in.'

There followed a few squeaked protestations.

Foster laughed. 'He's a doctor, seen more

than you can show him. Let him in.' The last three words came sharply and the girl moved from the door.

The doctor pushed it open and stepped into the room. A second girl, naked, sprang from the bed and leaped to the clothes strewn on a chair where the first girl was grabbing some to try to cover her nakedness. The doctor looked over the top of his spectacles at Clay who, amused by the whole scene, lay back against the pillows.

'Hi, doc,' he grinned.

'You don't waste time,' grunted the doctor as the girls scurried from the room.

'They don't let you in a place like this,' laughed Foster. 'What brings you here? Ain't a likely place for you.'

'Like you arranged in Pine Bluffs, if things went wrong at any time this was a place you might hole up.'

'So?' said Clay. 'Things did go wrong thanks to Porter bringing in that bastard Millet.'

'Yeah, but maybe they aren't as bad as

they seem.'

'How come?' Clay was curious.

'I suppose the last thing you know about is when your horse crashed into Porter.'

'Stupid coot,' muttered Clay. 'How is he?'

'Dead.'

'Dead?'

'He was about to take a shot at you after you knocked him over but Cheyenne got him first.'

Clay nodded thoughtfully. 'And he and the Wells boys put it over the sheriff.'

''Fraid not. At that point they held the upper hand but Richie Collins stepped in, wounded the Cheyenne Kid and from then on the law had them.'

'So things are bad.'

'Not like you think. Millet and Collins took 'em to Little Rock but only after Cheyenne had time to recover and I said when. That gave me time to get word to Sheriff Dutch Harper in Little Rock. I knew he'd had dealings with the Wells boys in the past. He got the right circuit judge, Judge Wilson, with the result that the Wells brothers and Cheyenne only got two years. Millet had waited in Little Rock for the trial, tried to protest against the sentence and to bring up the happenings in Pine Bluffs but the judge would have none of it. Millet and Laura Porter are on their way to Montana and Richie Collins has been made Sheriff of Pine Bluffs.'

Clay's agile brain had been assimilating and assessing the news as the doc gave it to him.

'Anyone else know about the railway?' he asked.

'Not that I know of.'

'Millet tell anyone?'

'Only likely person is Collins.'

'How can you be sure?'

'Look at it this way. The railway's proposed route is a secret for a year. Let that secret out to any of Pine Bluff's citizens and they'd try to take advantage of it. Millet wasn't a man to allow that. He'd keep his secret but, as he was leaving, I figure he'd tell Collins, because of his position as sheriff.'

'I figure you're right. So we could move back in,' grinned Clay, his voice tightening with anticipation.'

'Now you're talking,' grinned the doc. 'We can still pull this one off.'

'You old drunk, you still figure you won't retire in poverty.'

'I sure do. Won't be long before I have to retire. At everyone's beck and call twenty-four hours a day is getting me down. And I need my whisky. And I want to afford it after I retire.'

'So you threw in with me.'

'Don't forget you wanted me.'

'Sure I did. Your position enabled you to get a lot of information and I was grateful. We had that town tied up. You'd have never have been without your booze and the railway job was going to add to it.'

'It still can.'

'I need guns to back me,' Clay pointed out. 'And don't say pick 'em up here. I wouldn't trust any of the coyotes who hang around here, except maybe on a one-off job. I know the Wells brothers and the Kid and can work with them and they know me and know just how far they can go.'

'We can have them again.'

'Two years you said they got. The railway secret will be out in a year. We need to muscle in on that land before then.'

'They'll get remission for good behaviour.'

'Eighteen months. Still too late.'

'Yeah,' agreed the doctor, 'but we needn't wait for eighteen months.'

Clay eyed the doctor. 'That can only mean one thing, a gaol-break.'

'Sure.'

Clay grinned. 'I figure you have something in mind, you old reprobate.'

'Not in detail, you've the brains for that. But I figure Dutch Harper won't be beyond giving a little assistance.'

'We want no one else in on this railway business,' warned Clay.

'He needn't be. Harper likes to keep the right side of the law but is not averse to closing his eyes, or dropping a hint, if it's made worthwhile and he's not implicated.'

'So how's Harper going to fit in?'

'I came here by way of Little Rock and had a few words with Harper.'

'You sly old fox, you've got everything arranged,' grinned Clay.

'No. Just made a few enquiries about the prisoners.'

'So,' prompted Foster.

'He sees they get to the Pen. If they earn remission they'll know in ten months and, he as the sheriff who took them in, will be expected to move them from the Pen to another gaol to serve out their time to eighteen months.'

'And in that move there could be an attempt to break out, with Harper putting up a token resistance.'

'Sure. But it will have to look genuine or Harper won't play and he'll want well paying, with an assurance that he won't ever be implicated.'

'Sounds feasible.'

'Right. You work out the details.'

'You'll have to let me know where and exactly when the prisoners will be moved. I'll leave you to get me that information and to get Harper to agree.'

'I'll see to it and I'll get word to the Wells boys and Cheyenne. We don't want them messing up the possibilities of a remission.'

'Good. And tell them they'll be back working for me, with plenty of cash to spend. Ten months gives us a nice time to let things simmer down in Pine Bluffs and then we can take the townsfolk by surprise when we return. They'll soon be eating out of my hand again. Then we have two months to persuade the ranchers to part with their land nearest the town. Good work, Doc. Look after my interests in Pine Bluffs, I'll be back – soon!'

'You can't move back without your gunmen.'

'Don't intend to. It's nice enough here for ten months,' said Foster with a knowing twinkle in his eye. 'You staying, Doc?'

'Just tonight. Said I'd be back in four days. I'll be a day late through coming here via Little Rock. Didn't decide on doing that until I'd left Pine Bluffs.'

'Book a room here for the night. Want one of the girls?'

Doc peered over the top of his spectacles wondering if Clay's question had a touch of sarcasm in it. 'I could if I wanted,' he rapped back, 'but I'd rather have my bottle of whisky.'

'Right,' smiled Clay. 'I'll see you in the saloon shortly. I have some unfinished business here. Just tell the girls I'm waiting. They'll be next door.'

The doctor made no comment. Clay pleased himself. He had achieved what he had come here for. He was satisfied that his future would be devoid of poverty. Now he'd relax with a bottle for the rest of his time in Lonesome.

Six

Dutch Harper stared hard at the prisoners when they were brought into the guard room at the Penitentiary. They were no different to the day they had stood trial in Little Rock ten months ago. Maybe it was because Doc Warren had got word to them that all would be arranged for a break-out during their move from the Penitentiary.

'Right, move lively there.' Dutch's voice was hard. 'We have a train to catch.' His was a show of using his authority. He turned to the senior guard. 'Papers all ready?'

'Sure,' came the reply. The man pushed three papers across the table.

Harper glanced at each in turn and then signed them. The prisoners were now his responsibility. 'Given any trouble?' he asked.

'No,' replied the guard. 'Came here with a

111

damned hard reputation but they've been model prisoners. Guess they figured the hard time they'd get if they stepped out of line.' He grinned knowingly with just a touch of sadism in his eyes.

'They'd better continue that way if they know what's good for them,' said Harper in a voice which was a make-believe threat to the prisoners for the benefit of the prison guards and his own deputies. He examined the handcuffs which held the prisoners' hands behind their backs. Satisfied, he said, 'Let's go.'

The deputies moved quickly out of the room into the small courtyard at the opposite side of which lay a heavily studded door set in huge double doors forming the gateway in the high outer wall of the prison. The prisoners followed and were immediately flanked by prison guards while Sheriff Harper brought up the rear.

The group hurried quickly to the studded door which was opened by the senior guard. Harper's deputies stepped outside and positioned themselves one on each side of the door so that they could watch the prisoners as they came out.

'Hold it!' rapped one of the deputies when the prisoners had moved forward a couple of yards. They waited for Harper.

'Move,' he snapped as he stepped outside.

The three prisoners were looking around, drawing deep breaths into their lungs.

'Hold it a moment, Sheriff,' said Joe Wells. 'This sure is nice after being cooped-up in there.'

'You heard the sheriff. Move,' snapped one of the guards, shoving Joe forward roughly with the butt of his rifle.

Joe stiffened. Tension gripped him. He swung round, his eyes glaring enmity at the deputy. The man met his gaze without flinching but he had the comfort of a rifle pointing at a handcuffed man.

Harper sensed the tension. He knew Joe had a quick temper if provoked. He must cool the situation quickly. Nothing must go wrong or he could not play his part in the plan revealed to him by Doc Warren.

'Calm it!' rapped Dutch harshly. 'I want no trouble, from anyone, that goes for deputies as well as prisoners.' He looked hard at the deputy who had done the shoving. 'Don't throw your weight around unless it's necessary. These men are being moved from the Pen because of good behaviour, don't provoke them into going back. They deserve the chance to have their remission.'

The deputy smarted under the rebuke but said nothing. Joe straightened and eased the tension out of himself.

'Right,' said Dutch. 'The station.'

The prisoners and their escort brought curious glances from the people going about their normal business.

Reaching the station they went to the end of the platform at which Harper knew the front of the train would stop and where he knew a coach had been reserved for them.

Leaving the prisoners under the watchful eyes of his deputies he made a pretence of casually scrutinising the other people waiting for the train. Ten minutes later when the train arrived he instructed his deputies to see the prisoners into the carriage while he made a quick inspection of the rest of the occupants of the train. As far as his deputies were concerned this was a precautionary measure against any possible attempt to secure the prisoners' release by someone on the train. As far as he himself was concerned, Dutch was noting the people in case of any possible interference once the rescue was put into operation.

Satisfied, he returned to the carriage. The prisoners were seated one behind the other and his deputies were behind them.

'I'll be in here with the prisoners,' said Dutch addressing his deputies. 'I want one of you to ride on the platform between our carriage and that to the rear and the other one in a similar place up front.'

The two men nodded and moved off to take up their positions. Dutch checked that they were both in view through the glass panel in the doorway. Satisfied, he settled himself more comfortably in his seat. So far all had gone well but the hardest part was to come. He felt a little nervous about it but reassured himself that Doc Warren had promised that nothing would go wrong so long as he played his part straight down the line.

The train moved off amidst much hissing of steam.

'Hi, Sheriff,' Pete called over his shoulder. 'It's mighty uncomfortable sitting like this with our hands fastened behind us. Can't you unfasten them?'

Harper glanced both ways along the carriage. His deputies still stood in view. 'Be sensible,' he answered quietly. 'How would it look if your hands were free when the rescue was made? Anything out of the ordinary would look suspicious and I've got my future as a sheriff to think about.'

Pete grunted. 'All right. So long as you don't start thinking that future is more important than our release.'

Harper said nothing but eased the disconcerting feeling he had by standing up and stretching. He fished a watch from his pocket, glanced at it and returned it. Another fifteen minutes. He licked his lips nervously. He hoped everything was ready. Nothing must go wrong. His deputies must be taken by surprise. He had done his part by placing them where they were.

The train rumbled on. Harper sweated with nervous tension. The prisoners relaxed knowing that there was nothing they could do until the moment of rescue.

The sheriff glanced at his watch again. Five minutes had passed. Hell, time went slowly. He pushed the timepiece back in his pocket. The deputies! Were they still in position? He could see the deputy at the front of the carriage. He shuffled round on his seat to check the man at the rear. Damn! Where was he? Harper bit his lip. He half-rose from this seat then slumped back with relief. The deputy had moved back into view. The sheriff fished for his watch again.

The train gave a jerk. Hastily he rammed his watch back into his pocket. The train ran smooth, then jerked again. It slowed and the shuddering continued until there was a screech of metal against metal as the brakes were applied even more firmly.

Harper was on his feet, his gun drawn. He glanced out of the windows, first one side and then the other. He had to put on a pretence of being in command of the situation for the sake of his deputies.

He saw them move from his view to lean from their platforms and look ahead of the train. The man at the rear of the coach reappeared and opened the door into the carriage.

'Wagon across the line,' he called.

'What!' Dutch feigned his surprise. 'All right, get back out there and keep your eyes peeled. It might be nothing but you never know.'

The deputy turned and was gone.

Harper positioned himself so that he had the prisoners covered with his Colt, his back to the rear of the train.

The deputy at the front of the carriage

opened the door. Harper started. What the hell? He didn't want this man in the carriage.

'Wagon across the track. Looks as if it's broken down,' the man reported.

'All right, all right,' snapped Harper. 'Get back out there in case it's a plant.'

The man swung round, startled by the sharpness in the sheriff's voice but he figured with three gunmen under his care, Harper had a right to be edgy.

The deputy had no sooner left the carriage than the door at the rear of the compartment crashed open and two men, with bandannas covering the lower halves of their faces bustled in. 'Freeze!' yelled one of them as Harper swung round. 'Drop it!' Harper dropped his Colt and the second man pushed himself past to run to the front of the coach where his sudden appearance took the other deputy by surprise. The lawman never knew what hit him and never felt the push which sent him pitching off the platform, to join the other deputy in the dust beside the rail track.

'Unlock 'em, Sheriff!' ordered the man with the gun, as his companion returned to indicate that the second deputy had been taken care of.

Harper recalled the shirts. These men were already on the train when he had brought the prisoners on board. Whoever had planned the escape, and it must have been someone other than Doc Warren, had done it thoroughly; deputies placed so these men could eliminate them easily, himself with the prisoners so his own integrity could stand scrutiny from the authorities.

His hands shook as he unfastened the handcuffs with the prisoners grinning their pleasure at the smoothness of their rescue.

'Hurry it up,' ordered one of the gunmen. Cheyenne was free. 'On your way. Get to the wagon.'

Cheyenne needed no second bidding and was soon followed by Pete.

'Handcuff the sheriff,' the man instructed Joe. 'And use another pair to fasten him to the seat.'

Joe soon had Harper secured. 'Figure you'll have an alibi, Sheriff. Thanks for your help. So long.' He started down the carriage, paused, held up the key for the handcuffs and dropped it on a seat.

When Joe stepped down from the carriage he saw a horseman with two riderless mounts while another kept the train covered with a rifle. He guessed the occupants of the train were also covered from the other side. As he ran for the wagon he was aware of his rescuers hurrying to the two horses.

Cheyenne and Pete pulled him into the wagon and the driver sent the team of horses into a fast run along the trail to the east. As soon as the wagon crossed a rise and disappeared from view one of the men guarding the train fired into the air signalling to the men on the other side of the train that it was time to leave. They put their horses into a pounding gallop and were soon lost in the rise of dust, which billowed behind them as they headed north.

Balancing themselves to cope with the

sway and bounce of the wagon as the driver kept his horses stretched in gallop, the Wells brothers and Cheyenne laughed and yelled congratulating each other on their escape.

Joe edged his way forward and climbed on to the seat beside the driver while Pete and Cheyenne lowered themselves to sit on the floor of the wagon. It was a bone-shaking ride but that did not bother them, they were only too pleased to be free.

After a four-mile dash, the driver slowed the horses to a steadier pace and after a further mile turned the wagon in a wide curve until they were on a track heading back parallel to the way they had come.

'Hi, what's this?' demanded Joe, looking at the driver with some alarm.

'I'm only following instructions,' came the reply. 'We were seen heading east from the train, the fellas who got you out headed north so I figure when the law gets organised they'll start looking for you in the wrong places.' He grinned and sent the team into a quicker pace.

'Maybe it makes sense,' agreed Joe.

After a mile, he left the trail and followed a track until, after half an hour, it dipped into a hollow. The driver slowed the horses once again. Joe detected an alertness come to the man.

'Something wrong?' he queried.

'Hope not,' grunted the driver. 'Supposed to be met at the water.' He indicated the stream which flowed across the bottom of the hollow.

'Can't see anyone.' Joe was suspicious. He glanced back at his brother and Cheyenne. 'Keep your eyes peeled. Supposed to be met.'

The two men positioned themselves so that they could scrutinise the tree-lined stream.

Reaching the bottom of the hollow the man halted the wagon beside the ford.

'What now?' asked Joe. He felt naked and exposed without a gun.

'We wait.'

'But, hell we're easy targets...' Joe started to protest.

'We wait.' The man rapped his words

123

sharply. 'I follow instructions and get well paid for doing so. I ask no questions.' He eyed Joe. 'But someone was mighty anxious to terminate your sentence.'

Joe made no comment.

With each passing minute the tension in the escaped men rose. They became uneasy. This waiting in an exposed position was not to their liking. They were anxious to be on the move. Had something gone wrong? Had Foster's plans come unstuck?

'I'm going to take a look,' Joe nodded towards the top of the hollow.

'Sit tight!' rapped the man. 'I was told not to let you move from here!'

'But I want to know...'

The man frowned darkly as he looked at Joe. 'You go, but I'll tell you, if I get a signal and you're halfway up that slope I don't wait. I was given instructions to obey any sign immediately.'

Joe grunted with annoyance but sat still.

'Someone coming along by the stream. To the left.' Cheyenne's whisper came sharp and clear.

All eyes turned to the direction he had indicated. Nothing. Then a slight movement. The three escaped prisoners tensed. An animal? More movement.

'A horse,' said Pete quietly.

Before there was any more comment a rider broke from the cover of the trees. He stopped immediately he saw the wagon.

The Wells brothers glanced at each other nervously, but their apprehension was suddenly dispersed when the man called. 'All clear, Charlie!'

The driver of the wagon raised his hand in acknowledgement and sent his team across the stream to climb steadily out of the hollow. In the meantime the rider had disappeared in the direction from which he had come.

Once out of the hollow the driver put the horses into a steady motion. Ahead the land lifted into hill country and once they were among the hills the driver took a side trail which twisted and turned along a narrowing valley until it split into five more which pierced the heightening hills. Charlie pulled the wagon to a halt.

'This is where you get off, fellas,' he said.

'What?' The three men were surprised.

'There's no one here,' said Joe. 'What's the idea?'

'I told you I just follow instructions. You get off here.'

Joe, Pete and Cheyenne looked questioningly at each other. No one moved.

'What do you do?' asked Joe looking at Charlie.

'I go.'

'Leaving us here?'

'Yeah.'

'Leave us here, no horses, no guns, nothing?' protested Cheyenne.

'It's worked out right so far hasn't it?' snapped Charlie, irritated by the non-trusting attitude.

He eyed Joe. 'It's as well you stayed on the wagon back there, isn't it? Taking a look, like you wanted, could easily have left you stranded.'

126

Joe muttered his agreement. He looked at his two companions. 'Guess we'd better do as we're told.' He stood up and swung to the ground.

His brother and Cheyenne jumped out of the wagon.

Charlie nodded at the three men. 'Now you're acting sensible. So long.' He did not wait for any acknowledgement but sent the horses on their way, anxious to be back in his own saddle and rid of the wagon where it would never be discovered.

The three men watched it disappear and listened to its creaking and rumbling grow fainter and fainter until they were left with only the silence of the hills.

'What now?' muttered Pete.

'Wait,' said Joe.

'Weird place to be waiting,' returned Pete glancing round him.

'What the hell's Foster playing at?' grumbled Cheyenne. 'I like to know what's going on.'

'Sure, we all do,' agreed Joe, 'but everything's gone right so far. He must know what he's doing and he must have his reasons for doing it.'

'Where the hell are we?' asked Pete.

'Don't know,' replied Joe. 'There's nothing we can do but wait. Guess we may as well take it easy,' he added, sitting down on a rock.

His companions followed suit and an uneasy silence from the towering hills wrapped itself around them.

Irritation which comes with inactivity slowly permeated Pete. After twenty minutes he jumped to his feet. 'To hell with Foster. I'm getting out of here.'

'Cool it, Pete,' rapped Joe. 'Where are you going and how? You ain't got a horse, you ain't got a gun.'

'I can wait.' Cheyenne's words came with a cold slowness. 'If Foster wants us out of the Pen he must have something pretty big in mind. I'm willing to wait.'

'That's right,' agreed Joe. 'And whatever it is has to happen in the next eight months or he may as well have waited until we came out of the Pen legal like.'

'Yeah,' said Cheyenne. 'Foster's stuck his neck out to get us out of gaol so it…'

All further speculation stopped as a noise from one of the valleys brought Joe and Cheyenne to their feet beside Pete.

The noise intensified.

'Horses,' muttered Cheyenne. 'Ridden.'

'Better hide,' said Joe.

The three men moved quickly behind a huge boulder and peered cautiously round it in the direction of the unseen riders.

Tension built, with the sound of hoofs getting louder.

A rider, leading three horses, emerged from the valley.

'It's Foster!' cried Joe and stepped from behind the boulder closely followed by Pete and Cheyenne.

They hurried to meet Foster with smiles on their faces.

'Sorry to keep you waiting boys,' Foster called as he halted the horses.

'Think nothing of it, Clay,' replied Joe. 'Thanks for all you've done.'

'Think nothing of it,' said Clay, sliding from the saddle. 'Everything go all right?'

'Sure did,' grinned Joe.

'Sorry for all the precautions but I wanted to cover every possible track. I don't think the law will get on your trail. And there's nothing to connect Harper or myself with the escape.'

'Harper know what it's about?' asked Pete. 'Just thinking, he could talk.'

'He won't,' said Foster. 'I've paid him well, besides I have a hold on him about which you nor anyone else need know. He's played his part. Now I want you to take a slice of the action.' He studied the faces of the three men as he was speaking and he knew they were already back into their roles as gunmen for Clayton Foster. Now he could trust them with more information.

'Where are you operating?' asked Joe. 'Must be big to risk breaking us out of gaol.'

'It is,' said Foster. 'The name of the place is Pine Bluffs!'

Seven

'Pine Bluffs!'

Joe's astonishment was reflected on the faces of his companions but Clay noted that there was also a gleam of anticipated satisfaction in Cheynnne's cold eyes.

'Sure, why not?' grinned Clay.

'Ain't it getting to be a bit hot for us there?' put in Pete.

'Why should it be? Millet left soon after your trial and Richie Collins is sheriff now.'

'Collins!' The word hissed from the Cheyenne Kid as the name conjured up the revenge he wanted.

'Yeah. He shouldn't cause you any trouble,' pressed Clay.

'What about the townsfolk?' asked Joe. 'Will they accept us again?'

'I figure the majority will and the rest will

131

come to understand that we are benefiting the town by bringing trade and cash.'

'You been keeping a check on things?' asked Joe.

'Sure. I had too much to lose in Pine Bluffs. My interests have been looked after while I've waited in Lonesome for the day when I could return.'

'Lonesome!' Joe eyed Clay with some curiosity. 'If you were in Lonesome why didn't you recruit some other gun-slingers and move in on Pine Bluffs before now?'

'Because I wanted you. You knew what I had created in Pine Bluffs. I was embarking on another scheme which needed gunmen of your calibre to back it when Millet appeared. When you went to gaol I…'

Clay's tone made Cheyenne curious. 'Could you have had anything to do with our light sentence?' he broke in.

A faint smile flicked Clay's lips. 'Yeah. As soon as I knew Millet was taking you for trial at Little Rock I was in touch with Sheriff Harper and Judge Wilson.'

'You got something on those two?' queried Joe.

'Just let's say they owed me a favour.'

Joe nodded but made no comment. Instead he asked, 'But why today, why not wait until we'd finished our...'

'Because that would have been too late,' Clay cut in. 'I have some knowledge which must be acted on in the next two months before it becomes generally known.'

He offered no more explanations and the three men knew it was not wise to ask at this moment.

'So, what are we waiting for?' asked Cheyenne. 'Let's get to Pine Bluffs and that coyote Collins.'

'Hold it, Cheyenne,' said Clay. 'You notice that today there have been elaborate precautions following your escape from the train. I arranged them so that I made absolutely sure that your trail hadn't been picked up. It hasn't, so now we move to Lonesome until the time is right to take over in Pine Bluffs again.'

'What about the men who pulled the rescue?' asked Pete.

'They're all trustworthy as far as I am concerned,' replied Clay. 'I vetted them while I was in Lonesome and when I proposed bucking the law this way they were eager to do so. They've been well paid for the job. They don't know why I wanted you free and they won't ask. Just be careful that you don't say anything while you're in Lonesome.' Clay paused. There was no comment. 'Any more questions?' he asked.

Joe looked at his two companions. They shook their heads. 'Guess not,' he said. 'Thanks for what you did.'

Clay nodded. 'Play along my way and you can have some rich pickings. Let's ride.'

They reached Lonesome in the early evening and Foster soon had his three gunmen settled in the hotel and enjoying the things they had missed in gaol.

The following afternoon Clay and Joe were sitting on the sidewalk outside the hotel when the gunman suddenly started and sat upright in his chair. Clay saw the surprise on Joe's face and followed his gaze along the main street.

'That's Doc Warren from Pine Bluffs,' gasped Joe.

'Yeah,' agreed Clay casually. 'He'll be coming to see me.'

Joe turned and looked hard at Clay but the puzzled expression disappeared as he realised what lay behind that remark.

'So it's the doc who's been keeping an eye on things in Pine Bluffs for you,' he said.

'Yeah.'

'What you got on him?' queried Joe, curious about Clay's power.

'Nothing,' replied Clay, 'but it's mighty useful to me to know that a man who likes his drink is close to retirement and doesn't fancy it without cash.'

The doc pulled up in front of the two men, and slid from the saddle. He eased his limbs.

'Ain't got used to a horse yet?' grinned Clay.

'Never shall,' snorted Doc Warren. 'Pesky creatures. Sooner you get back to Pine Bluffs the better I'll like it – no more riding to do.' He stepped on to the sidewalk and acknowledged a greeting from a smiling Joe Wells. 'All went well, yesterday?'

'Sure did,' replied Clay.

'Authorities puzzled by the whole thing,' said the doc.

'You've had enquiries in Pine Bluffs?' asked Clay.

'Yeah. It was natural. That's where Joe, Pete and Cheyenne last worked, though the lawman that came with the news reasoned that you were unlikely to return there. I made sure I got to the sheriff's office when I saw this lawman ride in and I supported his theory. I figure that Collins sees it that way too, though he seemed a mite nervous when the lawman broke the news.'

'Fine,' laughed Clay as he imagined the scene in the sheriff's office. 'So when do you reckon we can move in?'

'Day after tomorrow.'

'Why not tomorrow?'

'I figure it might take the attention away for a while if you got someone from Lonesome to ride north and spread the word that Joe and his brother had been sighted up there and someone else could head east and give out a report that the Cheyenne Kid had been seen.'

Clay grinned. 'You're already earning a bigger share for your retirement, Doc. I'll fix it. How about the rest of the townsfolk, how are they feeling?'

'Well, the majority will be glad to see you back. Trade's gone down since you left and although they didn't take too kindly to having the likes of Joe around they agreed that they never stirred up trouble deliberately.'

'I guess you must have been spreading the right opinions in the right places,' commented Clay. 'You deserve a drink.' Clay pushed himself from his chair. 'Coming, Joe?'

The three men made their way to the saloon where the doc soon forgot about having to ride a horse again. But the necessity came painfully home to him when Clay, an hour later, informed him and Joe that they would ride in half an hour.

Joe left the saloon to alert his brother and the Cheyenne Kid while Clay arranged for the false sightings to be made, and the doc had another drink.

As they broke camp the following morning, after spending the night on the trail, Foster started to lay his plans. 'You ride on into Pine Bluffs, Doc, we'll be in tomorrow as you suggested.'

'Hell, another night in the open,' muttered Pete, 'when I could have had another night snugged up with that little gal in Lonesome.'

'Kill it, Pete,' rapped Joe. 'We're here on more serious business.'

'How right you are,' supported Clay. He eyed Pete. 'There'll be plenty of time for all the girls you want, when we get this job finished, and it's got to be through within a couple of months.'

The Cheyenne Kid took it all in without saying a word as he checked his guns. His mind was settled on a sheriff called Collins.

When they parted company with Doc Warren, Clay broke away from the main trail into Pine Bluffs and circled to bring them on to the hills overlooking the town. He studied the land for a short while before he spoke.

'Right, I'll give you the set-up. You can see from here that a strip of land about a mile wide follows the river. It's going to become very valuable and I want it.'

'How come?' queried Joe.

'The railway's likely to come that way. The decision will be announced in two months' time. I knew this when we were here before but somehow Millet heard of it and figured that was my big play.'

'And no one else knows?'

'It had been a tight-kept secret. Still is but I had my way of finding out. Better you don't know about that.'

'Where does the doc fit in?'

'I let him in on it because of his influence with the townsfolk. He put it about that I was good for the town. I was doing nicely. Then I heard about the possibility of the railway coming and the land to the south of the town, which the railway would have to use, could be worth a lot of money. I tried to buy it but the ranchers wouldn't sell so I brought you in. I had plenty of time; the public announcement from the railway was a long way off so I figured it better to consolidate my position in town and let the folks get used to you being around. Then that fool Porter had to bring Millet in.'

'Two ranchers will be concerned,' commented Joe eyeing the land in question, 'Ben Young of the Circle C and Lew Hardin of the Running W. I figure they won't be likely to sell their land; you'd be taking their access to water.'

'Right,' agreed Foster. 'So if they won't sell they'll have to be persuaded.' He eyed the three men and knew that they had got his meaning. 'Any questions?'

'What about any dissenters among the townsfolk?' asked Pete.

'They'll have to be dealt with,' replied Foster. 'But I'm figuring on no opposition when they see that I'm bringing money to their town and they all benefit from that.'

'What about the sheriff?' asked Cheyenne.

'I think I can leave you to take care of him,' replied Clay.

'Sure.' Cheyenne gave a short nod. He looked at his two companions. 'You two understand that. He's mine.'

'A pity that bastard Millet isn't here, I'd have him for Jake,' hissed Joe, remembering the death of his brother.

'We can head north when we get this settled, find him, and then Mister Millet will be no more,' said Pete, his voice filled with venom.

'Right, so we camp here the night and ride into Pine Bluffs in the morning.'

'I see the doc's back,' commented Richie Collins as he looked out of the window of Kate Robson's room in the Golden Cage.

'So you've noticed that he's been spending

quite a bit of time out of Pine Bluffs during this last year,' said Kate, coming beside Richie and observing the doctor climbing off his horse.

'And that for a man who hates horses except between shafts,' mused Richie. 'You know, when Cap Millet left he warned me to keep an eye on the doc.'

'Think he could be up to something?' Kate laughed. 'That sounds ridiculous. What trouble can the doc start?'

'He was a crony of Foster's,' said Richie.

'I know, but I reckon that was only because Foster was a good buyer and the doc likes his drink.' She looked thoughtful. 'But,' she went on, 'the doc has been doing a lot of moaning about how the town is missing Foster and the money he brought in.'

'That's maybe because he's lost someone to buy his drinks.'

'Say a thing often enough and people come to believe it.'

'Sure but what would be the point in this case? Foster's been long-gone and not likely to come back.'

'He's still drawing money from the town.'

'Didn't know that. How come?'

'He still owns the Golden Cage. I bank the takings and I presume the same thing is happening with his other properties.'

Richie looked thoughtful. 'Has he never had any of it transferred elsewhere?'

'Not to my knowledge, but then I wouldn't know, the bank would do the transfer.'

Richie was curious. 'Figure I'll pay the bank manager a visit.' He left the Golden Cage and a few minutes later was confronting the bank manager with his query.

'Oh, come, Collins,' said the manager with a half smile, 'you don't expect me to divulge the transactions of my customers.'

'If it is a matter of interest to the law.'

'Why should this be of interest to the law?'

'Foster was run out of town because of his activities, if his money's not been drawn off it could be a sign that he'll be back.' Richie's voice sharpened. 'And if that's likely I want to know.'

'He was good for the town,' snapped the bank manager. 'If that old fool Porter hadn't interfered, folks here would be coining more money than they are.'

'You still haven't answered my questions,' rapped Richie.

'No and nor shall I,' returned the bank manager.

Richie, realising he would get nowhere, swung on his heel and hurried out of the bank.

'Another one wishing Foster was back,' snapped Richie irritably when he reached Kate's room. 'But I'd bet my last dollar that none of Foster's money has left Pine Bluffs.'

'So you think he'll be back?'

'He has every reason to be.'

'But he won't have…'

Richie's shout interrupted Kate. 'And the Wells brothers and the Cheyenne Kid have been busted out of custody.'

Kate stared wide-eyed at the sheriff. 'You think they'll team up again?'

'Foster could have been behind their

break-out. There had been some careful planning. Besides why spoil their chances of remission when they hadn't long to serve?'

'Unless they were wanted for something big,' mused Kate.

'And who else but Foster would think that way? He's the organiser, the Wells boys and Cheyenne just hired guns.'

'So you think they could be heading here?' Concern for Richie showed on Kate's face.

'Yeah and it could be a bigger deal than just owning this town, or why risk busting them out of gaol?' Richie looked thoughtful. 'I wonder if Cap knew anything?'

'Such as?'

'I don't know. Wish I did, then I might have some idea if Foster and the gunmen are likely to return.'

'And Cap's too far away to ask.'

'Guess I'll have to do some poking around. Maybe start with the doc.'

'Be careful, Richie. You're on your own.'

Eight

Richie straightened from the papers he was examining at his desk in the sheriff's office. The distant murmur was unusual. The buzz of people coming together in the quiet of Pine Bluffs was not a usual occurrence. He had heard it before but, since the day he and Cap Millet had escorted the Wells brothers and the Cheyenne Kid out of Pine Bluffs, a situation had never arisen which brought people gathering together on the main street.

Richie pulled himself to his feet and crossed the office quickly. He jerked the door open and stepped on to the sidewalk to meet a growing intensity in the noise. His body stiffened and he held the scene sharply in his mind.

Four men rode at a walking pace along the main street, but these weren't any men. They were the four men whom Richie hoped were far from Pine Bluffs but whom he had half-expected to return. Even so their appearance shocked him. But he was startled as much by the reception they were getting.

As word spread of their arrival, more and more people flowed on to the sidewalks. Many called out a greeting which was amiable and in lots of cases they left the new arrivals in no doubt that things looked good for their return.

Richie's lips tightened. He felt a clammi-ness come to his hands and a sickening feeling grip the pit of his stomach. His mind flashed back to the time when as Cap's deputy he had faced a mob bent on lynching the same men as they were now greeting. Then he had hesitated to act and learned from Cap's actions how he should have cooled the situation quickly and kept the initiative with himself. Maybe he should do the same now.

He watched the four men halt their horses in front of the Golden Cage. He saw that several of the crowd, now milling in front of the saloon, cast glances in his direction, wondering if their sheriff was going to take any action against the new arrivals.

Three of the riders swung to the ground but the fourth sat on his horse. Richie held the cold stare of the Cheyenne Kid until he broke it off and swung from the saddle to follow his fellow riders into the saloon. The crowd poured in after them.

Richie swung round and went back into his office. He took down his gunbelt from the hook on the wall and buckled it round his waist, checked the hang of the holster and tied the leather thong to hold the gun more firmly to his thigh. He picked up his stetson, crammed it on his head and left for the saloon.

He gave himself no time to consider the situation and what its outcome might be. Three of these men were gaol-breakers and as such he should arrest them but he might have to bide his time before he could do that. The fourth still had property in Pine

Bluffs and had every right to return but the fact that he was accompanied by three hard gunmen with whom he had previously tried to take over the town smelt of trouble.

Richie crossed the street quickly, stepped on to the sidewalk and pushed through the batwings into the saloon. The new arrivals were at the bar surrounded by well-wishers who figured they had been better off when Clayton Foster was operating in Pine Bluffs. The sheriff weighed up the situation in a quick glance and walked purposefully towards the new arrivals.

He reached the back of the crowd and pushed two men out of the way without a word. Immediately they saw it was the sheriff who had manhandled them word of his presence went through the crowd like a prairie fire and brought a silence spreading quickly through the saloon. The crowd parted, making a pathway for the sheriff to the four men who still leaned on the mahogany counter. Richie saw that they were watching him through the long mirror behind the bar.

He stopped two paces behind them. Kate Robson who was standing beside Foster turned and her eyes flashed a warning for Richie to be careful.

'Howdy, Foster. In Pine Bluffs for long?' Richie controlled his voice, hiding the nervousness he was feeling. Foster did not answer immediately but took another sip of his whisky, all the time keeping his eye on Richie through the mirror. He put his glass on the counter with a casual, deliberate gesture and turned round slowly.

A faint smile flicked his lips and his eyes gleamed with an enjoyment of the situation. 'Well, if it ain't the sheriff come to greet us.' He held out his hand.

Richie ignored it. 'I asked you a question, Foster,' he rapped. His eyes, though intent on the man, took in the fact that the Wells brothers and Cheyenne all turned round to lean back on the bar while Kate moved away from the group as did the customers.

'Don't know,' replied Foster. His hesitation was momentary before he added, 'Of course

151

I know, I'm here for good.'

'You ain't welcome here,' said Richie coldly.

'Didn't look that way to me from the way these folks greeted us when we rode in,' laughed Foster.

'They ain't learned their lesson from last time,' retorted Richie.

Foster smiled. 'That may be your opinion but it seems to me that they figure they were better off before I left.'

A murmur of agreement rippled round the crowd.

'So you figure you can do the same?'

'Sure, why not?'

'And end up running again?'

Foster's face darkened. He did not like to be reminded of that day. 'I'm here for good,' he rasped, 'and if you're thinking of turning me out, forget it. You ain't the right. There's nothing that says I can't settle in Pine Bluffs if I want to. I've still got property and interests here. If you know what's good for you, Sheriff, you won't deny me a private visit in

152

your office in half an hour.'

Richie knew he had no legitimate right to run Foster out of town and maybe it would be best to hear what Foster had to say.

'All right,' agreed Richie, 'but there's one thing you're forgetting; you're riding with known gaol-breakers and it could be assumed that you'd helped in their escape from the law.'

'Come now, Sheriff, do you think I'd do a thing like that?' mocked Foster. 'I met up with them on their way here so we rode together.'

'If we're gaol-breakers are you going to arrest us?' The words came with a whip-like challenge from the Cheyenne Kid. He straightened from the bar and his hand hovered close to the butt of his Colt.

'I will when the time comes,' rapped Richie, his eyes watching the Kid like a hawk.

'Make it now!' The Kid was clearly goading Richie into drawing his Colt, wanting to erase the memory of being outsmarted by Collins.

Richie's eyes narrowed. The challenge was out. An oppressive silence settled over the room. The crowd, tense, waited and watched. Richie knew he could not back out.

'Hold it, Kid!' The words rapped from Foster, and split the tension. The Kid eased his stance. Richie kept his eyes firmly on him, alert for any trick to throw him off his guard. 'I want to talk to the sheriff and I can't do that if Collins is dead.'

Annoyed that he had been deprived of his revenge, Cheyenne swung back to the bar and drained his glass.

'Ease it, Sheriff,' said Foster, emphasising the last word with a touch of mockery. 'I'll see you in your office.'

Richie relaxed, nodded, and left the Golden Cage.

Half an hour later the door of his office opened to admit Foster. Clay crossed the floor and sat down on the opposite side of Richie's desk.

'You handled yourself well with Cheyenne,' commented Clay as he laid his hat on the desk. Richie said nothing but merely nodded. He was curious as to why Foster wanted this interview. 'I liked it. You could be useful to me.'

'What you getting at?' queried Richie suspiciously.

'First of all, you've no right to run me out of town. Secondly the town benefited when I was here before.'

'I'll not deny that you brought money in,' cut in Richie.

'Right, and the townsfolk liked it.'

'They'd lost their spunk and pride in themselves and the town especially after you brought in the Wells brothers and Cheyenne.'

'Oh come on,' laughed Foster. 'Who cares about the pride of a town like this?'

'Some do.'

'Don't get noble, Collins. You've heard the folks today. They can see money returning to their pockets. They're glad I'm back. You run against me and they won't back you.'

Richie knew that Foster could well be right. Cap had given some of the pride back to the

155

townsfolk, made them believe in themselves again but he had seen all that evaporate with the reappearance of Foster and his promises.

'Maybe you will bring more cash to the town but there must be more to it than that. You were doing that before you brought in those gunslingers. They're back with you so you must be wanting to take up where you left off. And that I don't like. Besides, gaol-breakers have to be arrested.'

'Not worth your while trying that, Collins. Remember the odds are three to one and I figure even on a one-to-one basis you wouldn't be quick enough. So my advice is forget all about arresting them. Ride with me.'

Richie leaned back in his chair and eyed Foster shrewdly. 'And what might that mean?'

'Nothing really active, just don't buck me or enquire into anything in which I'm involved. Oh, you'll have to put on a pretence of doing so, but it's easy to turn a blind eye.'

'That smells as if you're going to ride on

the wrong side of the law.'

'I'll be frank with you. It does and what I have to do has to be achieved within the next two months. And I'd rather have an understanding with you so I won't have you yapping at my heels right at the start.'

'And you need those gunmen?'

'I figure I will. It just might happen that I won't if some people see sense but I have them here if I need them.'

'So, I guess it was you who engineered their escape. You wanted them out for the purpose of being your trouble-shooters.'

Richie took Foster's denial as confirmation of his part in the gunmen's break from the law.

He realised that he was in a corner. He figured if he called for help from the townsfolk he would be in the same position as Cap found himself except that he would stand absolutely alone. It would be him against the rest of the town. Probably his only friend would be Kate Robson and there would be nothing she could do to help him. But he couldn't let Foster run this town and now by his own admission Foster had bigger things in mind which he was prepared to carry out with the help of guns. But how could he stop it?

Richie needed time to think.

'You're asking a lot of me,' said Richie.

'No. It only…'

'I'm a lawman, remember.'

'So?' Foster shrugged his shoulders. 'Don't have a conscience. Think of yourself. The job doesn't pay well, I know that. Ride with me and I'll treble your pay and I'll see that there are some nice bonuses.'

Richie raised his eyebrows in surprise. Foster had given him the opening he needed. 'Well, now that's putting a different light on the matter.'

Foster smiled. He had always figured that there was no man who could not be bought one way or another. He'd never had a chance to try it on Cap Millet, Cap had seemed willing to play along with him but then had moved a mite too quickly. Maybe Richie had learned from Cap. He would need to be watched but that would be easy with the Cheyenne Kid nursing a grudge. 'Anyone who sees things my way will find me generous,' said Foster. He pushed himself from his chair. 'I'm glad we understand one another. It's been well worthwhile talking to you. See you.' He picked up his stetson and with a nod at Richie turned and left the office.

Richie sat pondering over his conversation with Foster for the next hour. Try as he would to figure out what big scheme Foster had in mind he could not find an answer. He racked his brain, carrying it back to Cap and Mal Porter, trying to remember if they had ever said anything which would give him a clue as to what Foster was up to.

He heard a noise grow in the street and when he peered from the window he saw Foster and his sidekicks leaving the saloon. As they rode away in the direction of the livery stables, the crowd dispersed and the quietness of the earlier part of the morning returned.

Richie left his office and used the outside staircase at the back of the Golden Cage to reach Kate's room. She opened the door to his knock.

''Come in Richie,' she said with some relief. 'You gave me a scare; I thought you were going to draw on Cheyenne.'

'I would have done if Foster hadn't stepped in,' replied Richie as he sat down.

'Richie, be careful. The Kid was goading you.'

'I know, but I couldn't have done anything else but stand up to him if it had come to a showdown. I'm the law here.'

'I know,' said Kate sympathetically. 'What are you going to do about them? They are gaol-breakers.'

'What can I do?' said Richie helplessly. 'I'll get no backing from any of the townsfolk. The doc sure prepared them for Foster's return. You saw how he was welcomed today.'

'What's he up to?' mused Kate.

'Something big but I don't know what,' replied Richie and he went on to tell her of his interview with Foster.

'So, are you going to play along with him?' queried Kate.

'Looks as though I'll have to pretend to,' said Richie. 'For a while at any rate, to see if I can find out what he's scheming.'

'Why not send for Cap?' suggested Kate. 'String Foster along until Cap can get here.'

'I can't do that, Kate. He left me here as lawman. I can't go whining to him every time I have some trouble.'

Kate said no more. She saw that it would hurt his pride if he had to resort to that. 'Richie, do be careful. And let me know if there's anything I can do.'

'I think all you can do is to keep your eyes and ears open. And thanks, it's good to know I have one friend in town.'

Nine

During the following week Richie saw little of the Wells brothers or of the Cheyenne Kid. They spent most of their time out of town and though they always appeared in the Golden Cage during the evening they kept very much to themselves except when Clayton Foster joined them for a while.

Foster had some magic about him and Richie was one of the first to admit that trade in all aspects of the town looked up. Ranch hands came into town more often and from further distances as the news that entertainment of every sort was improving and expanding in Pine Bluffs. With news travelling fast the same week saw the men from a cattle drive come into town, a forerunner of what could be a lucrative trade. The citizens did not disguise their pleasure at the up-turn which Foster's presence and business acumen had brought.

Richie realised that to do anything to upset this pattern would bring enmity from the townsfolk. To try to arrest the Wells brothers and Cheyenne would antagonise Foster which would fuel opposition from the influential people of Pine Bluffs.

To all outward appearances Richie played along with Foster until one day Ben Young of the Circle C rode into town.

The sound of hard-ridden horses brought Richie out of his chair to look out of the window of his office. He saw the bulky, broad-shouldered rancher heading, with three of his riders, straight towards the sheriff's office. There was something in their approach which alarmed Richie. He smelt trouble. He moved to the door and was on the sidewalk when the four riders hauled their horses to a halt in front of him.

'Collins,' boomed Ben as he held his sweating horse from twisting around, 'I want you to arrest the Cheyenne Kid on a charge of murder!'

Richie gasped. His stomach churned. It had happened. He had known all along that sooner or later he would have to come face to face with the Cheyenne Kid. Now a charge had been thrown which he could not ignore.

'Come inside, Ben,' said Richie tersely. He turned before the rancher could say any more.

Richie wanted to hear what had to be said in private, not in front of a crowd which had started to gather, drawn by the grim-faced horsemen.

Richie held the door open. 'What's this all about, Ben?' he asked as he closed the door after the rancher had stomped into the room.

'Cheyenne shot one of my men,' stormed Ben. 'I've witnesses out there.'

'Now hold it, Ben. Let's hear this from the start. Cheyenne just didn't ride out to your place and shoot one of your hands.'

Ben eyed Richie suspiciously. 'Hi, you

ain't riding with the likes of Cheyenne and the Wells brothers?'

Richie stiffened at the implication. 'Hell no.'

'Well, what's the Kid and the Wells boys doing here? You should have arrested them for jumping gaol.'

'I know that, Ben,' replied Richie. 'But, hell, they ride for Foster and Foster is good blood for this town, at least that's what all the townsfolk figure. If I bucked him or his sidekicks I wouldn't get any support from anyone.'

'Well, you've got some support right now,' snapped Young. 'So let's get…'

'Hold it,' cut in Richie. 'There's more to it than that. Foster busted those men out of gaol because he wanted them for a special job and I want to know what that job is. That's another reason I've never moved against them.'

'Maybe I'm the special job,' said Ben.

Richie eyed him with curiosity. 'What do you mean?'

'Foster wants to buy land from me, not just any land; he wants it bordering the river.'

'What?' Richie's tone was disbelieving. 'But that would take your water away.'

'Sure. Naturally I refused. He offered a better price and when I still refused he tried to make some arrangement over access to the water.'

'And?' prompted Richie when Ben hesitated.

'I'd have been a damned fool if I'd agreed. The land would have been his and he could easily ignore the plan and shut me out.'

'What the hell does he want the land for?' puzzled Richie.

'Didn't say. He's not a rancher, besides the strip he wanted wasn't big enough. Unless cutting me off from water was an opportunity to force me to sell the rest of the land.' Ben shook his head. 'No, I'm sure that wasn't his reason. There's something else.'

'What about the killing?'

'We started getting trouble. Niggling things. Cattle spooked. Some found dead.

167

Corral fences broken down. Mustangs run off.'

'Horse thieves?'

'Wouldn't say so. We found the mustangs in a draw later. Early today three of my men surprised the Wells brothers and Cheyenne sneaking around the stables. They challenged them. Cheyenne shot Glen Baxter.'

'Self-defence?'

'Glen never drew his gun. The two men who were with Glen will swear to that. Cheyenne also told them that there'd be more if I didn't see sense.'

'Looks as if Foster's prepared to put pressure on you to get what he wants.'

'Sure. And I'll hit back if it's necessary but first I figured the law should have its chance.'

'Right,' said Richie. 'The Wells boys and the Kid have been spending a lot of time out of town…'

'Yeah, hitting at me,' cut in Ben.

'…been showing up in the Golden Cage in the evenings. But I'll take a look now.'

Richie picked up his stetson and started for the door.

When the two men stepped on to the sidewalk their attention was drawn by two riders approaching at a swift pace.

'Lew Hardin,' said Ben identifying his neighbour first.

'Trouble at the Running W as well?' Any further speculation was stopped as the two riders pulled their horses to a milling halt in front of the office.

Lew Hardin, tall in the saddle, glanced at Ben Young with a certain amount of curiosity but he eyed Richie much more firmly. 'I'm complaining, Sheriff. I've been suffering damage to property, horses run off, cattle missing during this last week. Couldn't figure it but today we identified the bastards – those gaol-breaking sidekicks of Foster.'

'Did the same to me,' said Ben Young. 'The Cheyenne Kid killed Glen Baxter this morning.'

'Hell!'

'Foster been at you for land?' queried Ben.

'Sure has. Land along the river.'

'And you refused to sell?' asked Richie.

'Sure did.'

'Must be playing for something mighty big if those gunmen were brought in to force your hands,' commented Richie.

'Don't know what,' said Hardin. 'The amount of land he wanted ain't that much but it would cut off my water supply.'

'And mine,' put in Ben.

'Right, let's see if we can get an answer,' said Richie with a determination which belied the apprehension he felt inside.

Richie started across the roadway to the Golden Cage and the crowd, which had gradually swollen in numbers, followed.

When he stepped inside the saloon, he stopped and surveyed the room. There were only about six people there. No Cheyenne Kid. No Wells brothers. No Foster.

He saw Kate standing at one end of the bar and took a step towards her, then stopped and returned to the sidewalk.

'All right, break it up. There's no one here,'

he called, feeling disgusted at the townsfolk who had obviously followed expecting to witness a showdown. 'Git,' he yelled again as there was only a reluctant movement in the crowd. He turned to Young and Hardin. 'I figure it better if you get on back to your ranches. I'll deal with them when they return.'

Ben hesitated. One of his men had been killed and he wanted to see someone pay. But he was a man who would give the law its chance. He nodded and made his way back to his horse followed by his men and by Hardin.

Richie watched the crowd disperse and waited until Young and Hardin had ridden out of town before he re-entered the Golden Cage.

Kate was waiting for him. 'The Kid shot Glen Baxter,' he said quietly.

'I know,' said Kate. She realised what must be going through Richie's mind. The showdown they knew would come one day was here. 'He and the Wells brothers rode out of town as they have done for the past week. If they follow the same pattern they'll be in here this evening.'

'Foster?' queried Richie.

'Rode out about ten.'

'Any idea where?'

'No.'

'The doc?'

'He was here when Ben Young rode into town. When he heard that the Kid had killed Baxter he was back in here quick asking if anyone knew where Foster was. No one did and the doc left.'

'The killing bothered him,' mused Richie, 'and he wasn't sure if Foster knew about it?'

'I'd say he was a mite upset.'

'Maybe killing didn't figure in whatever is going on between him and Foster and he didn't like it.'

'If the Kid didn't shoot in self-defence he maybe did it on purpose.'

Richie eyed Kate. 'You mean to force me to act against him.'

'Well, you outsmarted him when you were

deputy and he said he'd get you one day.'

Richie licked his parched lips.

Kate recognised a desire to get out of a situation which he knew was being forced upon him but one on which he could not turn his back. She glanced at the barman and nodded. A glass of whisky appeared in front of Richie. His eyes met Kate's and he knew she knew how he felt. He reached for the glass and took a sip.

'Leave town, Richie,' Kate said quietly. 'It'll be some time before the Kid's back. You can be far away.'

Richie leaned on the counter and studied his glass. 'I can't, Kate, and you know it. Couldn't live with myself if I ran. Besides, I'd be letting Cap down. He left me in charge and...' His voice trailed away and he looked up and saw Kate's gaze fixed on the door. He had heard it open but had not really been aware of it. Now, that sound had stopped; the saloon had gone deathly quiet. 'It's the Kid, isn't it?' Richie asked quietly.

Kate nodded. 'I didn't think he'd come

until this evening,' she whispered. Her face had drained of its colour.

'Maybe as well,' said Richie and sipped at his whisky again.

'Hi, Sheriff! Hear tell you're looking for me.' The Kid's voice boomed with a challenge across the saloon.

Richie did not answer. He needed the Kid nearer. Any advantage in surprise which might have been his had gone, ruined by some loud-mouthed citizen informing the Kid of the happenings a short while ago in Pine Bluffs.

'Sheriff! I'm speaking to you!' Irritation snapped in the Kid.

Richie still took no notice.

The silence was suddenly split by the sharp rap of footsteps as Cheyenne started across the saloon. Richie glanced in the mirror behind the bar. The Kid came into view. He held no Colt. The footsteps got louder. When Richie saw that the Kid was where he wanted him he swung round. The Kid stopped.

'I was speaking to you!' Cheyenne's eyes

smouldered with annoyance. His lips set tight.

The two men held their eyes firmly on one another. Each watching for the slightest move towards their guns.

'You killed Glen Baxter?' asked Richie, his voice steady, cold.

'Sure. Going to do something about it?'

Richie was stunned for a moment. He had expected Cheyenne to plead self-defence. If the Kid had then the law would have had a way out. But he wasn't. He must have set this up on purpose to confront Richie.

'Then I'm going to have to take you in.' The words came quietly from Richie. His hand moved swiftly towards his Colt. It closed on the butt and in the same movement drew it from its leather. A loud roar blasted round the saloon. The sheriff's stagger was stopped by the counter. His eyes took on a disbelieving look. Another roar split the saloon. Richie jerked, doubled up. He tried to continue the movement with his gun but it seemed so heavy. His fingers closed on the trigger and with a roar the bullet blasted into the floor. Richie sank against the bar, pitched forward and lay still.

The stunned silence was broken by the crash of the door being flung open.

Foster followed by Joe and Pete Wells burst into the room.

'Hell!' Foster cursed beneath his breath. 'What the hell?' he hissed as he reached the Kid's side to see him standing smiling at Richie's body.

'He tried to arrest me for murder,' replied the Kid quietly, still staring at the sheriff.

'For Baxter, I suppose,' snapped Foster. 'I thought I told you no killings unless it became absolutely necessary.'

Cheyenne turned his head slowly and looked coldly at Foster.

'It was necessary,' he said quietly.

'Let's get out of here,' rapped Foster. He swung round, glanced with exasperation at the Wells brothers and hurried from the saloon. The three gunmen followed.

'Well, we ain't got any law to bother

176

about,' grinned Cheyenne as they joined Foster on the sidewalk. 'Reckon that'll make things easier for you.'

'It could bring repercussions from outside when word gets out,' replied a tight-lipped Foster. The situation needed retrieving somehow, and quickly. Hurrying footsteps on the sidewalk drew his attention. He looked round and saw the mayor, Jim Maltby, accompanied by Doc Warren, and Brooks, the newspaperman, coming towards them. No doubt they had been drawn by the sound of shooting. 'Maybe the answer's here,' he muttered half to himself.

'What's been happening?' queried Maltby.

'Sheriff drew on Cheyenne, but wasn't fast enough,' explained Clay.

'Reason?' snapped Maltby eyeing the Cheyenne Kid.

The Kid met his gaze with cold eyes sending out a warning not to be too nosey.

'Accused me of killing a cowpoke. Without hearing my reasons he drew on me.'

Maltby nodded. He glanced at Foster. He

had no wish to go against this man who, in bringing more cash into Pine Bluffs, was pushing money his way through extra trade in his store. He could turn a blind eye to queries if necessary.

'So we're without law,' Maltby said.

'Sure,' confirmed Foster. 'But needn't be for long. Cheyenne's proved himself a better man than the sheriff we had so I suggest you fix the tin star to his shirt. You three have the power to appoint him here and now. It will stop queries from outside and if anyone asks … well, you'll think of something plausible.' He eyed each of the townsmen in turn.

The doc pursed his lips and glanced at Maltby. 'Guess Clay's got something.'

Maltby nodded. 'Guess so.' He looked at the newspaperman. 'Brooks?'

'Good idea,' replied Brooks. 'Good stuff for the paper. Excuse me, gentlemen.' He turned and hurried away.

'Right,' said Maltby. 'You're sheriff, Cheyenne.'

The Kid grinned. 'That makes me feel

mighty important.'

The doc stepped past the group. 'Guess I'd better see about the body.'

Maltby nodded and left in the direction from which he had come.

'And I'll tell you what, Ben Young and Lew Hardin will find they can't buck the law too easily,' said Cheyenne.

Foster smiled. 'You catch on quick, Cheyenne. And I figure you have a couple of deputies here who'll back you.'

'No stopping us,' grinned Joe. 'This job will soon be tied up now and then I search for that bastard Millet. I ain't forgotten Jake.'

Ten

Laura walked on to the veranda of the long low ranchhouse and looked in the direction of her husband who, with two hired hands, was breaking some horses in a nearby corral.

Everything had gone well for them since leaving Pine Bluffs and Cap had resettled to a ranching life he had known long ago. He seemed happy and contented and Laura blessed the day that Cap had entered her life.

Her attention was drawn by a movement. A rider had topped the hill which rose gently about half a mile beyond the corrals. The rider put his mount down the slope but she paid him little attention until he approached the corral in which Cap was working. Maybe someone looking for work. She saw the rider stop and speak to one of the hired hands who was sitting on the corral fence. He must have called out for Laura saw Cap hand the long rein to the man beside him and cross the corral to the newcomer.

A few words were exchanged before Cap climbed over the fence and stared towards the house. As he drew near, Laura frowned. Something was wrong. There was a troubled seriousness on her husband's face. What had the stranger been saying to him to bring this reaction? Laura moved towards the veranda steps to meet Cap.

'What's wrong? Who is it?' she called as Cap neared the steps.

He came on to the veranda before he answered. He looked deep into her eyes for he knew that what he was about to say would upset her and he wanted understanding from her.

'He came with a message from Kate Robson,' said Cap.

'From Pine Bluffs?' said Laura, a cold hand clamping on her heart at the thought of the place.

Cap nodded. 'Yes. Seems the Wells brothers and the Cheyenne Kid were busted out of gaol when they were being transferred from the Pen. They turned up again in Pine Bluffs with Foster. The Kid killed Richie.'

'Oh, no.' Laura's gasp was drawn out.

She steadied herself against the rail for she knew what was coming.

Cap moved to her side and took her arm with a feeling of love and compassion for her for he knew she had already guessed what he was going to say.

'I've got to go, Laura. I've got to.' His voice was quiet but determined.

She looked up at him, anguish in her eyes. 'Why? You can do no good there. Richie's dead.'

'That's why. I put him in that job. I could have brought him here with us if I'd only thought. Instead I left him in a vulnerable position.'

'But you never expected Foster and the others to turn up again,' pointed out Laura, wanting to purge her husband of the blame he was laying on himself.

'True, I didn't. Seems they have and Foster's got the town in his grip. He's got its soul again.'

'Then let him have it,' cried Laura. 'What's Pine Bluffs to us? Nothing! It's a...'

'Laura,' Cap gripped her shoulders and pulled her gentle to him. 'I'd never be myself again ever if I did nothing about Richie and about Pine Bluffs and the men who are ruining it. Your father's efforts would be in vain.'

Laura nodded as tears welled in her eyes. She knew it was useless to try to protest any further. Her head sank against his chest and she sobbed.

Cap had the town of Pine Bluffs in sight but decided to hold back until it was dark.

He instructed the man who had brought the news to ride on into town and inform Kate that he would be in when it was dark and to be sure that the door was unlocked so that he could use the outside stairs to her room. Cap watched the man ride off as he settled down to await darkness.

Cap approached the town at a walking pace and kept to the back streets until he was at the rear of the Golden Cage. Securing his horse at the bottom of the stairs he climbed them two at a time. He eased the door at the top gently and stepped into the dimly lit corridor. A gentle knock at a door brought it quickly open.

'Cap!' Kate greeted him with a hug.

'Good to see you, Kate,' said Cap closing the door gently behind him.

'How's Laura?'

'Fine, thanks.'

'Didn't want you to come.'

'Right.'

'I'm sorry I had to tell you. Nearly didn't for Laura's sake but I figured you'd know one day and regret you had not known immediately.'

'Too true, Kate. You did right. Tell me all about it.'

'Sit down. I'll get you a drink.'

When they were seated Kate began her story about the killing of Richie.

'The Cheyenne Kid sheriff?' It was almost too incredible to believe.

'I reckon, from Foster's attitude when he rushed into the Golden Cage immediately after the killing, that he had wanted none of it but now that it had happened he turned it quickly to his advantage and got a hold on the office of sheriff. And Cheyenne is sure manipulating the law to suit Foster's purposes but his big drive is against Ben Young and Lew Hardin, don't know why but seems some land is involved. Not much, a strip along by the river. Seems as if Foster wants to cut them off from their water supply. But why?' Kate shrugged her shoulders.

'The railway,' said Cap.

'Railway?' Kate was puzzled.

Cap explained the situation. 'I got to know from a friend in a top position in the railway company. It was when I was looking for a reason for Foster wanting to run this town and be in on every activity. I couldn't tell anyone because it would have jeopardised my friend's position and future. But Foster must have got to know from some other source, that's when he brought in the Wells brothers and the Kid. It was obvious to me he intended at some time to bring pressure on the owners of the land so I moved and precipitated that showdown. I never expected Foster and his gunmen to return. I figured their sentence would be longer and there was no chance of them being free before the railway had closed their deal. I reckon the judge and the sheriff of Little Rock were fixed by Foster and that's how he knew about the transfer of the prisoners and arranged for it to be easy to get them free.'

Kate let out a low whistle. 'Sure is one whole big plot. You know, the doc, who doesn't like horses, took to riding frequently, it's stopped since Foster returned. I figure he kept Foster informed of the situation in Pine Bluffs.'

'You could be right.' Cap looked thoughtful. 'How are the ranchers standing up to

Foster's gunmen?'

'They've been bucked hard in all sorts of ways. But they've held out against selling their land to him. But of one thing I'm sure, Foster's going to press so hard that there'll be a showdown here in Pine Bluffs.'

'And it will be soon,' said Cap. 'A month's time the railway's intention will become public. Foster wants that land before then.'

'If Ben and Lew bring their cowhands riding in here for a showdown with Foster there'll be a lot of blood spilt. Those hands will be no match for professional gunmen.'

'Anyone in town I can count on?' asked Cap.

Kate shook her head thoughtfully. 'No, Foster's got it tied up even more than when you were last here. Folks like the money that's come into their pockets directly or indirectly through him.'

Cap nodded.

'There's only Luke Chilton. He was the only one I could trust to ride to you with the message.'

'If he's the only one, I won't involve him directly. What he could do is look after my horse. Can I stay here tonight?'

'Of course you can, Cap. I expected you to. I've made a bed up in the other room. I knew you wouldn't share mine as much as I might like you to.'

Cap smiled. 'Thanks, Kate. You're a good friend.'

She pursed her lips wistfully. 'Another time another place and things may have been different.'

'Could have been,' said Cap quietly.

Kate pushed herself from the chair. 'I'll tell Luke.'

'Just a minute, Kate. Are Ben and Lew likely to be in the Golden Cage tonight?'

'Doubtful. They've been in less since this trouble intensified.'

Cap nodded. He looked thoughtful, trying to form some sort of plan. 'Can you tell me anything about the movements of Foster and his sidekicks?'

'Foster has what used to be the Porters'

house. He's brought a couple of girls in there. Rumour has it they are from Lonesome.'

'Lonesome! That's it!' cried Cap. 'I'll bet that's where Foster hid out and I'll bet he organised the party to rescue his gunmen there. Go on.'

'Well, he's rarely seen before midday. Joe and Pete Wells and the Kid ride out early and are never back in town until late afternoon.'

'Any more details about their leaving in a morning?'

'They're using the sheriff's office and the cells as living quarters. One of them, generally Pete, goes for their horses.'

'From the livery stable?'

'Yes.'

'Good.' A plan was already formulating in his mind. 'Can you fetch Luke up here without drawing attention to him?'

'Sure,' replied Kate and left the room.

A few moments later she was back with Luke.

'You willing to do a couple of jobs for me?' Cap asked.

'You just ask,' drawled the long-limbed cowboy.

'My horse is at the back of the saloon. Can you get it looked after without anyone knowing I'm in town?'

'Sure thing.'

'Right, then ride to see Ben Young and Lew Hardin. Tell each of them I'm here. Tell them I know why Foster's pushing them through his three sidekicks and the matter will be settled in the morning. Tell them nobody's to know I'm here and that I'd like them to be in town early with their men just in case I need some backing. They must drift into town in ones and twos and place themselves strategically along either side of the main street. If all goes well I won't need them but there's no telling.'

'Sure will,' said Luke and started for the door.

'And, Luke,' Cap's call halted the cowboy. 'I'd like you at the livery stable, seven in the morning.'

'Sure thing.'

Eleven

Cap left the Golden Cage, early the next morning, by the back stairs, and hurried along the side streets until he was at the back of the livery stable. He lifted the sneck on the back door quietly, eased the door open and stepped inside. He closed the door and slipped a piece of wood into the sneck.

Only the movement of horses in their stalls broke the silence. Cap drew his Colt and hurried quickly towards the front of the building where he knew the stable man had made a room for himself. He reached the door and paused to listen. He could hear the man still snoring. Satisfied, he waited, his ears tuned to catch any sound from outside the building.

Ten minutes later he heard footsteps approaching. With gun raised he waited beside the door. Someone pushed at it and it squeaked open. The tension eased from Cap when he saw Luke.

He nodded and was about to whisper when a sleepy voice called from the room.

'Be with you in a minute. You're mighty early.'

A few moments later the door to the room opened and the stableman, hitching his trousers up, appeared.

'You sure change...' His voice faded and he stared wide-eyed with amazement when Cap thrust a Colt into his ribs.

'Yeah, Walt, I'm back,' said Cap. 'I've some business to finish off. Just don't figure on trying to do anything to please Foster or his sidekicks.'

'I wouldn't do that Mr Millet, you know me,' protested Walt.

'Sure I know you,' snapped Cap. 'You run with whoever does you most good and right now with your stable full I figure it's Foster.'

'Aw, come on...,' started Walt.

'Put him in there and tie him up,' cut in Cap with a glance at Luke.

Luke nodded. 'Turn right around, Walt,' drawled Luke.

The stableman hesitated, eyeing first Cap and then Luke.

'Move!' rapped Luke. His huge, broad hand clamped on Walt's shoulder and spun him round. In the same movement he pushed him through the doorway. A few moments later Walt was well and truly trussed.

'Thanks, Luke,' said Cap when Luke reappeared. 'You stay in there with him. I don't want you playing gunfighter when Pete Wells shows up.' Cap waved Luke's protests aside. 'I'll handle this.'

Luke knew it was no use arguing and he went back into the room but determined to back Cap if anything went wrong.

Half an hour passed before Cap was alerted by footsteps coming towards the livery stable. He positioned himself opposite the door so that daylight would flood on to him when the door was opened. He levelled his Colt.

The door was pushed open sharply.

'Walt!' The next utterance froze on Pete Wells' lips. His eyes widened with the unexpected shock. 'Millet!' His action moved into a swift flow automatically started when he was struck by the fact that the hated Millet, his brother's killer, was standing there.

He clawed at the butt of his Colt, diving towards the stall on his left. Cap was almost caught unawares by the speed of Pete's reaction. He had not figured on gunplay in this encounter.

Cap dived forward, firing as he did so. The bullet took Pete in the right arm just as his gun was clearing leather. Instinctively he continued the motion in spite of the pain which tore through his arm, but the direction of his aim had been spoilt and his bullet crashed harmlessly into the floor.

The door of the room burst open and Luke, with his Colt in his hand, tore out.

His sharp eyes picked up the situation in a glance. Two strides took him into a position from which he menaced Pete. The gunman, whose gun hand had gone limp, cursed, and let his weapon slip from his fingers.

Cap was on his feet quickly. He knew the shot could bring Joe and Cheyenne on to the street.

'Get Wells into the room and watch 'em both!' he called as he leaped to the door. He jerked it open and peered in the direction of the sheriff's office.

The street was still, as if it was on the brink of an explosion. Cap slipped out of the door. He moved swiftly to the cover of the next building, Doc Warren's surgery, from which he had a better view of his old office.

In his movement he had seen several men on both sides of the street and knew that the Circle C and Running W outfits were there as he wanted them. The town was bottled up should the townsfolk try to back Foster.

The door of the sheriff's office opened and

Joe Wells and the Cheyenne Kid stepped out. They glanced in the direction of the shot, trying to estimate whether it had come from the livery stables and if so had it anything to do with Pete. They exchanged glances and each knew the other thought they should investigate. They started along the sidewalk, the Kid checking the hang of his holster. A word from Joe and the Kid stepped from the sidewalk and moved across the street.

Cap watched them carefully and this move opened up a greater problem. The Kid, from his new angle of approach, would see him earlier than he had wanted. If he was quick enough he could use the alley and back street to come behind the two gunmen but he would have to be quick to make it before they reached the livery stable. That decision saved his life for as he turned there was an explosion from the other end of the alley and wood splintered in the wall beside his head as a bullet ripped into it. Cap moved sideways, seeing the would-be killer as a shadowy figure. Cap did not hesitate. He was taking no more chances. He fired twice and saw the man jerk, tumble backwards and lie still.

Cap glanced anxiously towards the main street. Joe Wells and Cheyenne would now be even more alert. He ran swiftly to the end of the alley.

'Doc Warren!' he gasped when he saw the dead man. 'You must have been playing for high stakes.'

He stepped past the body and ran to the next alley. He hesitated at the corner and peered cautiously round. No one. He raced along the alley towards the main street and was three-quarters of the way along when a figure stepped into view. In almost the same moment a shot was loosed off and the man disappeared back on to the main street. The shot whined past Cap. He dived for the cover of a barrel. Breathing hard from the exertion he weighed up the situation. The hoped-for surprise was gone, and he could be pinned down here by one man while the other investigated the position at the livery stable.

As if to confirm this assumption a hand swung round the corner and fired twice. Cap replied with one shot and immediately sprang to his feet and in a crouched run returned the way he had come. Half-way to the back street he dived to the ground close to the building on the right hand side. He was not a moment too soon as the alley thundered with the crash of gunfire again. Cap rolled over and returned the fire. Then he sprang to his feet and flung himself round the corner.

He raced on in the direction of the livery stable, pausing near the back door of the stable to reload his Colt. He listened intently but the only sound he heard was the distant hum of curiosity rising from the people who had come on to the main street out of lethal gunshot range.

Cap was about to move beyond the livery stable, in order to circle to the main street, when he heard the sound of a door being pushed open with caution. He figured it came from the door on to the main street.

Luke could be in trouble any moment. Suddenly the door crashed open and, in the instant he heard it, Cap launched his pressure hard on the back door. The sneck broke and the door flew open. Cap was through it and moving to one side in the same flow. He saw a figure silhouetted in the doorway at the other end of the stable. Joe Wells! The immediate recognition impinged on his mind and brought his trigger finger into action automatically. His surprise was complete. Joe jerked. Cap raced forward at a crouch, needing to be nearer for a more certain result. He fired again. Joe staggered as he squeezed the trigger. The gunman slumped against the doorpost and a glassy stare fixed his eyes as he slid to the ground.

Cap did not hesitate. He was past the dead man and out into the open before Cheyenne realised it. Startled by the unexpected gun-fire from the stable he had started across the street.

The sudden appearance of the ex-lawman froze Cheyenne in his tracks. His stomach knotted for a moment and then a calmness came over him. He faced Cap Millet in the open and he reckoned that gave him an advantage.

His confidence to outdraw the man he faced grew.

Cap had no sense of superiority. He knew the Cheyenne Kid's reputation and he realised he would have to be fast and judge the moment right. He straightened from the crouch he had adopted when he stepped out of the stable.

'You're the only one, Kid,' he called. 'Throw your gun down.'

'There's still Foster. He'll still need a gunman. The townsfolk will back him.'

'I think not,' called Cap. 'Take a look down the street. The Circle C and Running W have the town, and Ben Young's making sure Foster can't escape from Pine Bluffs a second time.'

'Like hell!' spat Cheyenne. 'I ain't falling for that one. Me turn around?' He laughed with contempt. 'And let you shoot me in the back.' Cheyenne's eyes narrowed. 'It's you they'll be taking out of here – in a coffin!'

Cap had been watching Cheyenne intently throughout this exchange. Cap suddenly saw the glint in Cheyenne's eyes change to the coldness of a deadly killer. There was a roar as two guns split the silence which had hung over Pine Bluffs since the moment Cap had stepped into the open. But in that split-second of awareness Cap moved sideways as he fired. He felt a searing pain tear through his shoulder and the impact swung him round. He fought to keep his balance, fought to bring his gun back again in his defence. But there was no need. The Kid in his confidence of out-shooting Cap had held his ground and taken fatal impact of Cap's aim.

The body sprawled in the dust.

Breathing heavily Cap stared at it for a moment. He straightened slowly and slid his Colt back into its leather. 'For Mal Porter and Richie Collins,' he whispered. He winced with the pain in his shoulder.

Then he was aware that pandemonium

had broken out. People were running in his direction, clamouring and shouting. He waited, holding his hand to his wound. Then Luke was beside him. 'You all right?'

'Sure,' said Cap. 'This'll soon mend. The prisoner?'

'He won't worry anyone for the moment,' grinned Luke.

'Thanks for your help.'

Before Luke had time to reply, Kate Robson, with concern in her eyes for Cap's wound, reached them. Almost immediately a crowd was milling around. The mayor, Jim Maltby, pushed his big frame to the front.

'You again, Millet, what's this all been about?'

'You let Foster take you over a second time,' snapped Cap in disgust. 'The first time Mal Porter was killed, this time Richie. When I heard about it I felt responsible, I'd left him as sheriff. But you bastards wouldn't back him. Didn't care as long as you were lining your pockets through Foster. Well he took you for a ride. Once he'd got his hand on the land you'd have paid.'

'Land? I don't know what you're talking about,' stormed Maltby.

'Don't tell me you didn't know about the trouble Ben Young and Lew Hardin were having.'

The mayor's reply did not come as the crowd gave way under the pressure of Ben Young pushing Clay Foster forward.

'We held him, like you said, Cap,' said Ben.

Cap nodded his thanks. He eyed Foster. 'It's over this time,' he said. 'Pete Wells is the only one left and he'll talk to save his hide. No doubt he knows about the railway, like I guess the doc did.'

'Railway?' Several people gasped the word.

'Yeah. That's what this is all about. That's why Foster wanted Circle C and Running W land along the river. That's why Foster wanted to control everything in Pine Bluffs so he could reap all the benefit the railways will bring.'

Cap felt the pain in his arm and winced.

'Someone get the doc,' called Kate.

'No good,' put in Cap. 'He was in on Foster's schemes. He tried to shoot me and I'm afraid it was him or me.'

'Let me attend to it,' said Kate.

Cap glanced at Luke. 'Will you see to the prisoners?'

'Sure thing,' drawled Luke.

'One of your men help him?' Cap asked Ben.

The rancher nodded. 'And thanks,' Ben added with a sign of agreement from Lew Hardin.

An embarrassed Jim Maltby eyed Cap. 'My apologies. I'm sorry for everything.'

'So am I, sorry about Mal and about Richie.'

'We still need a sheriff.' Maltby's statement was a half-query to Cap.

'Then find yourselves a good one. I'm going home.'

The publishers hope that this book has given you enjoyable reading. Large Print Books are especially designed to be as easy to see and hold as possible. If you wish a complete list of our books please ask at your local library or write directly to:

Dales Large Print Books
Magna House, Long Preston,
Skipton, North Yorkshire.
BD23 4ND

This Large Print Book, for people
who cannot read normal print,
is published under the auspices of
THE ULVERSCROFT FOUNDATION